A PERFECT CHRISTMAS DANCE

KRINGLE, TEXAS
BOOK 7

LORI WILDE

Edited by
KIMBERLY STRIPLING

EPIPHANY
ORCHARDS

CHAPTER 1

RYAN DANVERS BALANCED on the icy slats of the barn roof in his Roper cowboy work boots the chilly December wind whipping around the raised collar of his shearling coat.

He plucked a nail from his mouth and hammered a new shingle into place.

A windstorm swept through Kringle, Texas, last night and ripped off two dozen shingles clean off the barn—the same barn set to host the annual Danvers' Christmas Party in two weeks.

With his high deductible, it wasn't worth filing an insurance claim, so now, instead of party planning, Ryan was up here risking his neck patching the roof, knowing every dollar he spent on supplies dinged his paper-thin party budget.

"Dang it," he mumbled around the remaining nails in his mouth and wiped cold sweat from his forehead with a gloved hand.

What in Santa Claus' name was he doing?

The weight of the past perched like an anvil on his shoulders. Seven years ago, his parents died in a horrific car crash on Christmas Eve.

For the first five holidays afterward, he and his older sister Jenny stopped his parents' beloved tradition, too heartbroken and lost in their grief to consider it. Celebrating Christmas seemed wrong in a hundred different ways.

Then, two years ago, for the sake of the town and their own mental health, Jenny insisted they start up the party again. Their parents—especially their mother—loved Christmas, but to Ryan, the holiday was a reminder of everything he'd lost.

And he resented it, even as he moved forward for the love of his sister.

This year, however, Jenny was on bed rest, expecting her first baby. The doctor issued strict orders—no stress, no planning, no running around organizing a party.

That left Ryan in charge and as much as he loved Jenny, he begrudged the solo responsibility.

Okay, Grinch. Get over yourself. This isn't about you.

He shook his head and eyed the sky. The wind bit his face and burned the skin beneath his beard stubble. Thick gray clouds gathered heavy in the sky with the threat of more icy rain. In this part of Texas, it rarely snowed, but sleet? Oh yeah, that was a thing. Why did it feel like Christmas was plotting against him?

One shingle down, twenty-three more to go.

Mentally, Ryan calculated the cost of repairs and deducted it from the party budget he and Jenny set at the first of the year. Yikes. He was coming up way short.

Hmm. He could take the roof repair from the ranch budget, but then he'd be grappling for property tax money come January.

Wincing, he pounded in another shingle. Seriously, why did the Danvers have to single-handedly fund a big Kringle Christmas shindig just because of tradition?

Tapping into his personal savings was also an option but because of high interest rates, he'd stuck most of his disposable income into certificates of deposits and early withdrawal would cost him all his gains.

Honestly, if it were up to him, he'd cancel the whole dang thing.

But it wasn't up to him. Not really. The Danvers Christmas Party wasn't just a family tradition—it was also a pillar of the town's holiday celebration, and the town sorely missed it during their five-year hiatus.

Local businesses depended on their event. The exposure and sales home-owned companies made during the party kept them going throughout the slow winter months. Canceling the party would mean letting folks down.

And Ryan hated letting people down.

Thirty minutes later, he hammered in the final nail into the last shingle and glanced up as a familiar red pickup truck pulled into the driveway. Scott Finley, his brother-in-law and best friend, parked and got out. Ryan hooked his hammer through a belt loop of his jeans and picked his way across the roof to the ladder.

Scott walked over, tilted back his Stetson, and squinted up. "What are you doing?"

"What does it look like?"

"Like you've lost your ever-loving mind."

Ryan grunted. "You offering to help, or are you here just to state the obvious?"

Scott chuckled and stepped to the base of the ladder. "Looks like you just finished. Perfect timing on my part."

"What's up?" Ryan peered over the eaves at him. "My sister okay?"

"Jenny's fine. She sent me to check on you. It worried her that you were out here on your own since you gave the ranch hands two weeks off for Christmas."

"My sister has enough to worry about without fussing over me. Tell her I'm fine. Now step off, I'm coming down." He waved, shooing Scott away.

Scott moved back and waited until Ryan was on the ground. "How much are these repairs costing you?"

Ryan winced. "Don't ask. Choosing a high deductible seemed like a good idea at the time for lower monthly insurance premiums, but now..."

"Where you getting the money to cover it?" Scott surveyed the old shingles lying strewn on the ground. The wind had blown several into the branches of the old oak tree next to the barn.

"Our party budget." He blew out his breath. "I hated to dip into it, but no roof, no party. I'll have to find somewhere to skimp."

"People will get it." Scott bent and started

picking up the old shingles. "Hard times all around this year."

Ryan joined him. "Yes, and the budget was already tight since you and Jenny couldn't put as much into the kitty with the baby on the way."

"We're really sorry about that. I had no idea how expensive babies were. I took on extra work but—"

"Hey, no shade. I understand completely. If the party didn't mean so much to the town, I'd just pull the plug on the whole thing, but bringing the event back the way we did two years ago made such a difference in the community."

"For sure it was a morale booster." Scott bobbed his head and carried the armful of shingles he'd collected to the nearby burn barrel. "Everyone in Kringle was so grateful when you two started the party back up again, and no one more so than me."

The reinstatement of the Christmas party two years ago was what got Scott and Jenny back together after five years of estrangement when Ryan hired Scott, a contractor, to renovate the barn. In fact, Scott was the one who put those shingles on the roof in the first place.

Ryan trailed after Scott. The grass, still covered in frost, crunched beneath their boots. He stared at him the festivities were also about everything he still had—his friends, the people of Kringle, Jenny, Scott, and soon a new niece or nephew. The ranch.

Home. Family. Community.

If he canceled, he wouldn't just be giving up on the party, he'd be letting go of the values and traditions his parents tried to pass down to him and he wasn't ready to let go.

He turned toward the barn, the patched roof standing as a small victory, but it didn't make the heaviness in his heart any lighter.

Not this time of year.

CHAPTER 2

SOMETIME AROUND SEPTEMBER, Nina
Ellis decided the only gift she wanted for
Christmas this year was Ryan Danvers.

He didn't know it, of course. No one did. And
though Christmas Eve was fast approaching, Nina
still hadn't figured out how to make her wish come
true.

It wasn't as if she could order Ryan online and
have him delivered. Even if she could, she'd never
be able to afford him. He was way out of her
league. Her best hope would probably have been
Santa, but the jolly old man didn't exist.

Ha, ha, ha, and ho, ho, ho.

Nina sighed and kneaded the silky pâte à

choux dough, pressing and folding the way her grandmother taught her when she was ten. The bakery stretched unusually quiet for a December afternoon. Customers trickled in and out, but the holiday rush hadn't materialized, leaving her too much time to think.

About Ryan. About the bakery. About how everything teetered on the edge this year.

Ellis Early Eats was more than just a bakery since her grandparents, Garrett and Ellie, opened it in Kringle in 1981.

For decades, Gee was the town's only doctor, back before it became a tourist town, marketing itself to big-city visitors during the holidays.

However, it was Ellie who made the bakery the heart and soul of Kringle. She filled the shop with the scent of freshly baked bread, cinnamon rolls, cream puffs, and her famous kolaches, all while raising three children and keeping the books for Gee's practice.

Nina's parents took over the bakery when she was a teenager and Ellie got too sick to run it anymore.

Her folks expanded the menu and updated the equipment, bringing in customers from all over the county and beyond. The bakery thrived until they retired four years ago and moved to Arizona, leaving the store to Nina with a little help from Gee after Ellie passed away.

She loved working with Gee, but things had changed. Her grandfather, who once juggled patients and pastries with ease, had slowed down and so now the financial side of things fell on her shoulders, and with rising costs and fewer customers, she found herself swimming upstream.

The bakery once buzzed with customers during the holiday season, but since urban sprawl from Fort Worth pushed the big box stores closer to Kringle, she found it harder and harder to compete. People still loved the idea of homemade baked goods, but the convenience of picking up a dozen cookies or a pie at half the price from Costco was doing them in. Nina tried to adjust, offering catering services and custom orders, but even those were drying up.

She glanced at the shelves dwindling of supplies. Lately, debt piled up faster than customers walked through the door.

Ryan Danver's Christmas order was a lifeline— two hundred kolaches, a hundred cream puffs, twelve dozen cookies, fifty pies, and ten sheet cakes. The largest single order they had all year, and if she could pull it off, the income from it would keep the bakery afloat until the Valentine's Day surge.

Photographs of her family hung on the wall in front of her. A snapshot of her grandmother pulling a tray of freshly baked rolls from the oven, head thrown back, laughing, was one of her favorites. Gee sitting with customers at a table, his smile warm and inviting, another.

Her grandparents built this place on love and hard work. Letting them down felt like a betrayal, but she didn't know what else she could do. She worked sixty to seventy hours a week, with no time for a social life.

Not that she minded. She loved the bakery.

Her gaze drifted to a framed photo of Gee from last spring with his church group. Ryan stood beside him, smiling, his hand resting on Gee's shoulder. That day meant so much to her—Ryan and a few other church members had stepped in to drive Gee to his chemo treatments when Nina was too overwhelmed to manage every day.

Ryan showed up at the bakery the first day Gee needed a ride, wearing that shy smile, and offered to help.

"Figured it was the least I could do," he said. "Your grandfather used to give me and Jenny free cookies when we were kids."

Nina's heart ached with a gratitude so intense she could hardly speak. The way Ryan helped Gee into his truck, and made sure her grandfather was comfortable, plumping a pillow for his lower back and adjusting the seat for his long legs, stirred something inside her.

Every Sunday during church service, Nina looked across the pews at him, as he held the hymnal, and his deep voice rang out above the rest.

One morning, he turned his head and caught her staring. He flashed her a quick smile. She dropped her gaze, her face flaming, and spent the rest of the service keeping her eyes locked on the pastor.

Ryan was kind and generous, never making a big deal about the help he offered, never expecting anything in return. That was what made him so different. He wasn't just the handsome rancher every young, single, straight woman in town swooned over. He was a good man. The kind of man she dreamed of but was too nervous to pursue.

After finishing the pâte a choux, she put it the fridge to rest and washed her hands at the sink.

The bell above the door jingled.

Nina dried her hands on a kitchen towel and stepped into the storefront to greet the customer and stopped in her tracks.

Ryan Danvers.

Looking more handsome than usual.

He wore a Stetson, work boots, and a shearling coat. He gave her a smile, but his lips pressed tight, and the smile didn't quite reach his eyes. "Morning, Nina."

"Hey, Ryan." She kept her voice neutral, not wanting to give away her flaming crush on him, and pushed back a tendril of hair that escaped her messy bun.

They looked at each other, neither one speaking.

"Well," they said in unison, then laughed together.

"You go first," he said.

"No, no, you." She waved, alarmed at how fast her pulse sprinted.

Ryan glanced around at the empty bakery and winced. "Pretty quiet in here."

She shrugged as if the vacant tables were no big deal. "It's Monday morning. Past breakfast and not yet ready for the lunch crowd."

He cleared his throat.

She interlaced her fingers in front of her, rested her knotted hands on her apron at her navel, and waited.

"I... um..." He pressed his palm to his nape and shifted his weight. "Listen, Nina, there's something I need to discuss with you."

Her breath hitched and a weird hope jolted through her. She leaned forward. "Yes?"

"About my order for the party..."

"Do you want to add to it?" she asked.

He dropped his gaze. "Um, not exactly."

Her stomach fell to the floor and rolled around. She latched her gaze on to his face, trying to decipher his unreadable expression. "What is it? You need to change something?"

He pointed at a table. "Could we sit down?"

"Is it that bad?" Her laugh came out nervous, edgy.

He didn't smile, just moved to the table and sat. He took off his Stetson and settled it on the chair beside him.

Uh-oh. Nina flitted behind the counter, uncertain what to do. "Would you like some lunch? I know it's a little early, but I also know ranchers get up before dawn too. I just sliced some roasted turkey and baked fresh sourdough loaves. I could whip up my avocado and turkey sammie, no charge—"

"No." He shook his head. "Thanks, but I should get back to the ranch. I've got a long to-do list."

"Oh, okay." Not knowing what else to do, she walked over and pulled back the chair across from him, the legs scraping against the floor, the noise extra loud in the empty bakery.

He placed both hands, palms down, on the table and met her gaze with steady eyes. "I know we have a written contract for the order, but I wonder if you're open to amending it."

Nina pursed her lips and exhaled slowly, emptying all the air from her lungs the way Gee taught her to regulate her emotions. "What's happened?"

"The storm blew shingles off my barn roof and the repairs took a bite out of the party budget. I can't afford to pay you all at once and I was wondering if you accept some kind of payment plan."

He'd already put down the ten percent deposit she required for large orders. Nina opened her mouth, but didn't know what to say, and closed it again.

"If you can't do that, I understand, and instead maybe we could reduce the quantity of the order?" His eyes searched her face, and his mouth pulled down.

"By how much?"

He grimaced. "By half."

She gripped the edge of the table, trying to steady herself. "Ryan, I've already placed the order for the ingredients."

"I wouldn't ask if I had any other choice." He sounded exhausted, and the muscle near his right eye ticked.

"You're right." She forced a smile. "It's just flour, sugar, butter. I can use that on any recipe. Nothing special other than it's a larger than normal expense."

"I'm so sorry. Forget it. I'll figure something else out." He pushed back his chair and got to his feet.

Nina hopped up too, flashing back to Ryan helping Gee into his truck, carefully fluffing that pillow and settling it just so for her grandfather. "Wait. Let me see what I can do. I'll crunch some numbers and get back to you with a payment plan.

Folks in Kringle look forward to your Christmas party every year. It means a lot to the community, and it was sorely missed the years after your parents... well... we don't want a shoddy party, do we? We'll make this happen one way or another."

"Really?" He looked so hopeful Nina decided she would rearrange the entire solar system if he asked her to.

"Yes." She bobbed her head and brightened her smile. She had no idea how she'd swing it, but she'd find a way, even if she had to run a balance on her credit card.

"Thank you, Nina. I know our friends and neighbors will appreciate it." He picked up his Stetson and settled it on his head. "It means a lot to me and Jenny too."

She wanted to say something inspiring and encouraging but the words stuck somewhere between her heart and her lips. He stood so close to her. She ached to reach out and touch him, to comfort him, but manners and personal boundaries held her back.

"I better let you get to work. I'm sure the lunch crowd will be descending soon," he said. "Let me know what payment plan you can swing and be fair to yourself, okay?"

"I'll text you." Her smile froze to her face.

He tipped his hat and left, the bell jingling in his wake. She tilted her head and watched him saunter away, her heart beating too fast, her mouth too dry. If Santa were real, Nina knew exactly what she'd ask for this year.

A Christmas miracle.

CHAPTER 3

OUTSIDE ON THE sidewalk Ryan turned to look over his shoulder through the bakery's plate-glass window decorated with Christmas-themed clings.

Behind the counter, Nina arranged a tray of Christmas cookies in the display case. Her fingers moved with an unconscious grace, lifting each cookie and placing it just so. She wore a Chilly Willy-themed apron over a simple blue sweater, the fabric lightly flour-dusted. She looked happy, surrounded by the tools of her trade, and there was a peacefulness about her he envied.

Nina had the most gorgeous hair he'd ever seen. True midnight black that shimmered with hints of blue in the sunlight, and right now, under the soft glow of the bakery lights, it looked like she'd painted in red and green streaks as if the Christmas spirit had found its way into every strand.

Ryan had always noticed her hair and admired the way it usually fell in soft waves around her shoulders, even if today she had it piled into a loose bun atop her head. A few tendrils escaped, curling around her face, softening her features.

Captivated, he stared.

She leaned forward to place a few more cookies on the parchment-lined glass shelf, her shirt pulled tight across her back, revealing the gentle curve of her waist. Ryan recalled the way she'd smiled at him earlier, the kindness in her eyes, and something inside him ached. It wasn't just attraction, though that was definitely there, but something deeper, something he couldn't quite put into words.

He thought of the sandwich she offered him and the charming warmth of her sweet little bakery.

She'd proposed food and company. Why had he turned her down?

Scott was right. He spent too much time on the

ranch. Too much time alone. Ryan took a deep breath and pushed open the door.

Nina looked up from the counter, surprise flashing across her pretty face. "Back so soon?"

"Yeah," he said, feeling awkward. He swept off his Stetson and shifted his weight from one foot to the other. "I, uh, thought I'd take you up on that sandwich if the offer still holds. Turns out I'm hungrier than I thought, but I'm paying. I insist. You can't keep a business going giving food away for free."

She blinked, and those lovely pink lips curved into a welcoming smile, one that made his pulse spike. "I'm glad you changed your mind. C'mon in and have a seat."

He took the table he'd sat down at before.

"You want the turkey and avocado on sour-dough?" she asked.

"That sounds delicious."

"Cup of butternut squash soup to go with it?" She pointed to the posted chalkboard menu on the wall over the counter. "Soup of the day."

"Sure, sure, but I have one request."

"What's that?"

"You have lunch with me." He glanced around

the empty shop. "At least until the customers show up."

"Deal," she said, upping the wattage on her smile. "I did expect it to be slower today since there's an event going on at the Kringle Kandy Kompany. I think they've got food trucks over there."

"Oh, that's right," he said as she disappeared into the kitchen. "They're introducing a new holiday candy."

"Yep, even got a Fort Worth news crew showing up."

"Fancy that," he said.

She appeared in the doorway between the kitchen and storefront. "Sorry, I didn't hear you. What'd you say?"

"Nothing important... hey, do you mind if I come hang out with you in the kitchen while you whip up the sandwiches? That is unless there's some kind of health code violation."

"No, come on in. Just wash up at the sink and stay away from my prep station. I've got a little table and chairs back here where we can sit."

Ryan joined her in the kitchen, stepping to the huge stainless steel sink to wash his hands while Nina sliced the sourdough bread.

The kitchen was even cozier than the storefront, the air thick with the smell of yeast bread and cinnamon. Her sound system perched on the windowsill was playing the Christmas song, "Winter Wonderland."

Nina assembled the sandwiches. Ryan kept his hands clasped behind his back and studied the photographs lining the walls that captured family moments over the years—three generations of Ellises loving and cherishing this place.

"C'mon over." She carried two platters loaded with sandwiches, dill pickle spears, chips, and cups of butternut squash to the little wooden table set up in a little alcove between the commercial refrigerator and the ovens. "Water okay or would you like something else to drink?"

"Water is fine."

She poured two glasses of ice water, and they settled into their chairs. Nina passed him a napkin from the dispenser on the table and took one for herself.

Ryan took a bite of his sandwich. "Mmm, this is delicious. Do you make your own aioli?"

"I do," she said. "Buttermilk is my secret ingredient. I learned that from Gee."

"Props for Gee." Ryan lifted his thumb. Why

didn't he eat at the bakery more often? While the lunch menu was limited, it was spectacular, nonetheless. "How is your grandfather doing, by the way?"

"Great." She nodded. "Completely cancer-free at his three year checkup. I can't thank you enough for driving him to his chemo treatment."

"I only did it the once." Ryan shrugged. "I didn't mind at all. Happy to help."

"Well, we truly appreciated it, and the cookies I sent as a thank-you don't seem near enough."

"You didn't have to send cookies, but I sure did enjoy them." He patted his belly. "Just like I'm enjoying this soup and sandwich."

She pulled her bottom lip up between her teeth, and her gaze held his. He smiled at her, hoping he didn't make her nervous, because she was easy to talk to, easy to be around. On the sound system, "Winter Wonderland" changed into "We Wish You a Merry Christmas."

"Gee would be here right now if he wasn't playing in a dominoes tournament at the senior citizen center. He's in the finals and hoping to win a trip to Padre Island."

"I didn't know he was a domino sharp."

"Oh, yeah." She laughed. "Mostly, though, he

uses it as an opportunity to dispense free medical advice to his friends and competitors. Once a medicine man, always a medicine man, I guess. He's still got that bedside manner. People ask him for advice on everything from aches and pains to what kind of flour they should use for biscuits."

She was a talker. Ryan hadn't realized that. Nina made him think of his sister, Jenny, in that regard. All those words tumbling out while he listened and delighted in every second of her conversation. Her talkativeness didn't bother him at all. It gave him time to think. He didn't want to mess up.

"Miles had big shoes to fill when he took over your grandfather's practice."

"He did," Nina agreed, nodding. "But Doc Miles is doing great. He really cares about the community, just like Gee did."

Ryan took another bite, the flavors of the sandwich bursting on his tongue. He licked a bit of aioli from his thumb and caught Nina watching him, her eyes lingering on his mouth. He froze for a moment, then cleared his throat. "I wouldn't know. It's been a while since I've needed to see a doctor."

"Guess all that healthy living is paying off, huh?" she said, looking him up and down in a way that gave him trouble swallowing the last bit of sandwich.

He finally got the bite down, and it hit his stomach hard, as he fought a bout of unexpected nerves. Why was he anxious?

Her words weren't suggestive or a come-on. She was just a woman noticing a man. Paying attention. Maybe thinking about how hard he worked or the things he could do with his hands—rope a wild mustang, wrestle a steer to the ground, cradle a newborn calf.

Or his own baby—

Whoa! Where had that thought come from? Ryan shook his head, feeling as if this kitchen and Nina's food had cast a spell over him.

He had no plans to start a family.

Ever.

Jenny was enough, and she and Scott could populate Kringle with as many little Finleys as they wanted. He figured he'd make a terrific uncle. He'd never seen himself as a husband or a dad material. He and Jenny had the best parents ever, and Ryan learned what it meant to be a man from the father who'd raised him. The one he would miss forever.

Nina stared at him as if she expected him to

say something and he realized he'd lost the thread of the conversation.

"Your good health," she said. "Must be from ranching."

"Oh yeah, yeah, that." He dipped into the butternut squash soup garnished with crème fraiche. "Don't have a lot of time for excesses. Unless too much work counts."

"It can, for sure." She rubbed her hands up and down her crossed arms. "When I was plotting a career, I never thought I'd be setting an alarm to get to work by three a.m. My teen self would be horrified. It was trying enough putting in a couple of hours at the bakery before school back then."

Ryan nodded. "I hear ya. I got up early for football practice after chores, ready to go, and everyone else would be stumbling around the locker room like they'd just rolled out of bed."

"They probably had," she said.

He thought back to what Nina had said. "You still get up early on your days off?"

She laughed. "I do try to sleep in, but my body thinks I'm running late and shoves me out of bed by five, but at least it's not three, which is ridiculously early."

He was usually in the barn by five, but five

wasn't three, and Nina was right. That was a ridiculous hour. "I don't remember the last time I was up past nine."

"I generally go to bed at eight. The same time as my grandfather, which makes me feel old." She laughed.

It was a fluttery sound. Light and fun like a butterfly. Ryan's gut clenched. He wanted to hear it again.

"But at least I get to eat breakfast on the job," she said. "Though I probably should cut back on the pastries. I'm a sucker for our blueberry cinnamon rolls. Have you tried them?"

Ryan found himself about to say something about how good she looked, that the pastry didn't seem to be hurting her, but he shoved his mouth full of soup instead. It didn't keep him from thinking how nicely she would fit against him, however, and that simply wouldn't do. He refused to objectify her in any way.

"I haven't tried the blueberry cinnamon rolls, but you've just talked me into it. I'll take half a dozen home with me."

He pushed back his empty plate and soup bowl and stood to clear his place. From the musical playlist, George Strait started singing about Christmas cookies.

Nina cocked her head and peered up at him. "Ryan?"

He looked down at her beautiful heart-shaped face surrounded by tendrils of jet-black hair and a solid ache hit his chest. "Yeah?"

"Would you care to dance? This song is my absolute favorite Christmas tune."

CHAPTER 4

NINA HADN'T EXPECTED him to accept her invitation, and honestly, she couldn't believe she dared ask him to dance.

But when he set down the dishes he carried and reached for her hand, tugging her toward him with a playful grin, she didn't care how awkward she sounded, because here she was, in Ryan Danvers' arms, two-stepping through her grandparents' bakery kitchen in time to George Strait.

His grip was warm and steady as he pulled her closer, one hand settling on her waist and the other hand holding hers with just the right amount of pressure. The upbeat rhythm of "Christmas Cookies" filled the bakery, the rollicking tune bouncing off the tiled walls.

Ryan led her in a lively dance, his boots shuffling on the kitchen floor, his laughter joining hers. He guided her around the shining pots and pans hanging from cooking racks and twirled her with a mischievous smile.

A giggle bubbled up inside Nina as he spun her out and then pulled her back toward him.

She couldn't believe she was dancing to a song about Christmas cookies in her kitchen with the man of her fantasies. It was surreal, ridiculous, and absolutely perfect. Nina hadn't been this close to a man she had such a mad crush on in... well... ever.

The feel of his belt buckle bumping her hip bone and his thigh sliding between hers as he led her sent her hormones rocketing off the charts. She liked the feel of Ryan. His hand, his shoulder. Every bit of him.

But something in his eyes left her wondering if her Christmas wish should stay a secret between her and Santa.

Maybe this dance was enough, a fleeting moment she could cherish, but once he released her, would she ever get this close to him again?

Oh, who was she kidding? She hadn't dated much since college, and she'd graduated four years ago. Work kept her busy. And those few dates?

Casual. Conversations over burgers or chicken-fried steaks from opposite sides of a table. A movie. Walks around the town square.

Those dates hadn't involved a man grinning at her like she was special, his intense eyes locked on hers as he dipped her. The sudden move yanked a gasp from her lips and sent her grabbing on to his shoulders for balance.

He was quick, though, righting her in an instant and drawing her near again, still keeping time to the quick tempo.

She never imagined he could out dance Patrick Swayze, his steps light and sure, guiding her around the kitchen like it was a huge dance floor and not a small space crammed full with baking equipment.

"I'm starting to think you were just waiting for an excuse to show off your moves," she teased.

He grinned down at her, his hand at her waist. "Maybe I just wanted to see if you could keep up."

She peeked up at him through lowered lashes. "I think I'm doing pretty well, don't you?"

"You're doing great." His gaze held hers. "You're more than keeping up, Nina."

She stared into his eyes and her heart stuttered.

The song ended, the lively tune fading into a

quieter, slower melody, Frank Sinatra's "The Christmas Waltz."

They stilled, his hand still at her waist, hers resting on his shoulder. Neither of them moved away. The air between them charged with something unspoken, something...

Unnerved by the look in his eyes, Nina stepped back, brushed her bangs from her eyes, and looked away. "Thank you for the dance."

He nodded, his gaze locked on hers. "My pleasure."

The bakery fell quiet, just the hum of the refrigerator and the faint sounds of the town outside filtering in. The air between them pulsed with energy and a touch of Christmas magic.

In the storefront, the door opened, and the bell jingled.

"You've got a customer," he murmured but didn't move an inch.

"Yeah," she said.

He didn't let go of her hand right away. His thumb brushed over her knuckles, a slow, gentle motion that sent shivers shooting down her spine. "I should get going."

She nodded, her pulse racing.

He gave her a small, crooked smile and dropped her hand.

Nina felt the loss keenly, the distance between them too vast, too empty. He glanced around the kitchen as if waking up from a spell.

"Thanks for a nice time, Nina."

"Anytime, Ryan."

"Hello? Yoo-hoo. Nina, you here?" a voice called from the front of the bakery.

"Coming," she called out. To Ryan, she said, "You can leave through the back exit."

"Thanks." He tipped his hat, and then he was gone.

Leaving Nina hungrier than ever for a man she wasn't sure she could ever have.

———

Ryan stepped from the rear entrance of the bakery into the alley, the brisk air cooling his flushed skin.

He glanced back at the lighted windows—why? Was he expecting to see Nina watching him leave? But the glass reflected only his own conflicted expression.

Ego check, Danvers. It was just a dance.

Whew. Ryan left the alley and ambled around the corner to the street where he'd parked.

His pulse was still doing the two-step long after his legs had stopped. What had he been thinking? He went back in for her delicious turkey and avocado sandwich, not to spin her around the kitchen like some kind of a Christmas fool.

But she'd asked *him* to dance.

Why?

He'd noticed Nina before. Who wouldn't? But noticing wasn't the same as letting himself feel something. Now those feelings rushed in all at once, and good grief, they left him reeling.

Ryan leaned against the hood of his truck and blew out a breath, collecting himself before he climbed in and drove back to the Double D.

Nina Ellis was full of life, too talented to be tied to a town like Kringle, never mind that her family roots sank deep in the soil. And him? He was just a man doing his best to keep his head above water, weighed down by responsibilities and sad memories he couldn't shake.

"Ryan Danvers!"

Dang it.

He knew that voice all too well. Putting on a smile for propriety, Ryan turned to see Mrs. Claiborne heading toward him, her bright-red coat swaying in the breeze.

The older woman carried several shopping bags, her petite frame almost hidden by her over-sized load, but her blue eyes, sharp and knowing, peered out from under her wide-brimmed hat.

Ruth Claiborne had been his Sunday school teacher, his mother's good friend, and practically a third grandmother to him and Jenny. He'd grown up under her watchful eye, and even now, she had a way of making him feel like a little boy caught sneaking extra cookies at the church picnic.

"Afternoon, Mrs. Claiborne." He pushed away from the truck and moved toward her.

She shifted the bags, her hands clutching the handles. "What are you doing out here, sneaking around the back of the bakery?"

"Who said I was sneaking out the back of the bakery?"

She arched her eyebrows and gave him The Look. The one she gave the kids who fumbled their bible verses.

"Here, let me help you with those." He reached out.

She hesitated for only a second before relinquishing the shopping bags. "Thank you, Ryan.

My car's down the street. I ended up buying more than I thought, and those sacks were getting heavy."

He took the load from her, and it was hardly a strain compared to the hay bales he hauled on a daily basis. "What are you doing carrying all this alone? Where's Freddie?"

She waved a hand. "Freddie's got a domino tournament. He's in the finals with Garrett Ellis. First prize is a weekend trip to South Padre Island."

"You don't say."

Her eyes twinkled up at him as she adjusted her red fedora. "Besides, I'm not helpless, you know. I could have managed, but why turn down willing muscle?"

"True."

She linked her arm through his and guided him down the sidewalk. "So, what were you *really* doing in the bakery? And don't you dare try to tell me you were buying baked goods because before you took on my burdens, you were empty-handed."

Dang it, he had been empty-handed and after he'd promised Nina he'd pay for his lunch and buy some blueberry cinnamon rolls. He'd gotten so addled by their dance, he'd forgotten.

Ryan's cheeks warmed as he glanced back at the bakery and told the truth, just not all of it. "I went in to talk to Nina about the big order I placed for our annual Christmas party."

"Something wrong?"

"Yesterday's storm blew off the barn roof and I had to take the cost of repairs out of the party budget. I asked her if she would take payments. Didn't want to, but..." He shrugged, his gaze dropping to the sidewalk. "Turns out Nina's suffering too with those big box stores moving in closer to Kringle."

"Hmm." Mrs. Claiborne looked pensive. "I see. You and Jenny have always been so generous, hosting that party every year. Your parents would be proud, but you shouldn't have to shoulder the financial burden for the entire thing."

"The party's our family's Christmas gift to our friends and neighbors."

"And it's a much-appreciated tradition... oh, here I am." She stopped beside her Cadillac. "You know, your parents would want you to be happy, Ryan. They'd be proud of you keeping the ranch going, but they'd also want you to have a life. And by life, I mean dating."

Ryan's chest knotted. "I know. It's just..."

She opened the back door, and he settled the bags down in the back seat. "Yes?"

"It's complicated."

Mrs. Claiborne reached up to pat his cheek. "In case you're not picking up on what I'm putting down, I'm talking about Nina. You're single. She's single. You're both young and good-looking..."

"It's not that simple."

"It could be if you don't go deciding what's best for Nina without even asking her, and don't think you're not worth loving just because you're carrying a heavy burden. A burden shared is a burden halved."

The accuracy of her words jolted him, and Ryan forced a smile. "I'll try to remember that."

"Well, since you're not planning to sweep Nina off her feet, how about helping at the church? We're setting up for the Christmas pageant and we need all the hands we can get. There's a potluck afterward..." She studied him expectantly.

He might be busy, but it wouldn't kill him to be charitable. Especially to a woman who'd been so good to his mom. "What day?"

"The setup is Thursday afternoon at three, then the potluck at six. Since you'll be working, you don't have to bring any food unless you want to swing by and pick up something from Nina." Mrs. Claiborne winked and then shot a glance over her shoulder at Ellis Early Eats.

"I'll see you on Thursday," he said, not commenting on picking something up from the bakery.

"You're a good man, Ryan Danvers, but please don't let the past steal your future." Mrs. Claiborne's eyes took on a sad, faraway expression.

He nodded and swallowed past the lump in his throat. "Thanks for the advice."

She hopped in her car and tooted her horn at him as she drove away.

Mrs. Claiborne might be right, but knowing and doing were two different things. How could he let himself hope for something more when the cost of losing it would break him all over again?

CHAPTER 5

TUESDAY MORNING, five thirty a.m., the day after her kitchen dance with Ryan, and Nina couldn't stop grinning. Yesterday evening, she'd emailed him a payment plan for the party catering that suited them both and when he emailed back that she'd saved his hide, she felt positively giddy.

Okay, yes, there'd been potential... and sizzle. Lots of sizzle. More than Nina had dared hope for actually, but these cookies wouldn't bake themselves. She had work to do.

Focus, Ellis.

All four ovens hummed, the bakery toasty warm as Christmas music played, and Nina rolled out sugar cookie dough that had already rested in the fridge overnight.

She cast a glance over her shoulder at the table where she and Ryan had shared a sandwich and then two-stepped their way over the wooden floor. A giddy laugh pushed up her throat, and she reached for the snowman cookie cutter.

Oh wow. The guy she'd secretly been crushing on for years liked her back.

Or at least he seemed to.

Why had she waited so long to make a move?

Why? Because he'd been chin-deep in grief over losing his parents in a tragic accident, and the timing never felt right.

But now?

Time had passed. Things had changed.

She finished cutting out the cookies, arranged them on the baking sheet, popped them in a preheated oven, and then took out the tray of blueberry cinnamon rolls. She had half a mind to send a dozen out to the Double D as a thank-you to Ryan for the dance, but that felt a little too forward.

Nina set the cinnamon rolls on the sideboard to cool and mixed up the glaze for the cherry popovers cool enough to frost. Singing along with "All I Want for Christmas is You," she filled the pastry bag and piped on the icing.

When her dance with Ryan ended, and they'd

stood for a moment in the quiet kitchen, she'd thought that he hovered on the verge of dipping his head and kissing her. She'd pursed her lips and tilted back her head...

Even now, just thinking about it, Nina's cheeks heated.

Goodness! How she'd wanted him to kiss her.

Yoo-hoo, Earth to Nina. Did you forget the real reason Ryan Danvers strolled into your bakery?

Yeah, he wanted a payment plan. Maybe he'd danced with her because he felt backed into a corner. Perhaps it had nothing to do with liking her. Maybe he simply felt *obligated* because she'd asked him to dance.

Nina dropped the piping bag and slapped a palm across her mouth. She'd never considered that possibility. She wanted Ryan to like her back and so she simply assumed that he did. But what if it was all a ruse to get on her good side so she'd offer him an ideal payment plan?

She didn't think he was a manipulative person, but honestly, what did she know about him other than he'd smiled at her in church and had been good to Gee the time he drove him to his chemo treatment?

But when they'd danced, and his hand settled

on her waist, he'd held her as if she was something precious...

Unless she imagined it.

The smell of burning sugar yanked her back to the moment. Smoke poured from the lower oven.

"No! No! No!" She grabbed oven mitts and yanked open the oven door. A puff of hot air singed her forearm hairs. Hissing, she dropped the tray into the stainless steel sink, the cookies burned to crisps.

Darn it. In her woolgathering, Nina had forgotten to set the timer. Terrific. Already down a batch, and she wasn't even open yet.

No crying over burnt cookies. It was Gram's voice in her head, gentle yet firm. *Start again.*

Right.

Nina took off the oven mitts and let out a sigh. Okay, enough with thoughts of Ryan Danvers. He'd derailed her too much already.

A knock sounded at the front door.

Nina leaned out of the kitchen to peek into the storefront. The bakery didn't open for another fifteen minutes. Who was this much of an eager beaver at five forty-five in the morning? Nina squinted into the darkness.

She didn't recognize the well-dressed woman

huddled on the sidewalk, her frosted blond hair twisted in an elegant chignon. She wore a chic camel coat with knee-high black leather fashion boots. Definitely not from Kringle.

The woman spied her and waved.

Nina went over, unlocked the door, and opened it a crack. "I'm sorry, we're not open yet."

The woman's smile was polished and professional. "I know it's early, but I wanted to get here before the breakfast crowd claimed your attention."

Nina narrowed her eyes and snapped her fingers. "You were in here last month."

"I was." She nodded.

"You bought two dozen madeleines for your book club."

"Excellent memory. Your cookies were a huge hit, by the way." The woman extended her hand. "Katherine Brothers. May I come in?"

"All right, but if you don't mind, I'll keep working while you talk," Nina said.

"Not at all. I don't want to hamper you."

Nina pushed the door open wide and flicked on the dining room lights. "Come on in."

"Thank you." Katherine stepped inside, rubbing her palms together and giving Nina a bright smile. "I do appreciate your time, Ms. Ellis."

Nina moved behind the counter to grind the beans and start the coffee. Katherine trailed after her, scanning the bakery's interior. "Such a charming old building."

"Yes, Kringle built the town square in the 1890s, and all the buildings are still original, although the National Historical Society green-lighted renovation on most of them."

"And the bakery has been renovated as well?"

"Yes, my grandparents undertook that task when they started Ellis Early Eats." Nina added water to the coffee maker and sent a sidelong glance at the woman. What was Katherine angling at?

"That's excellent. You should be really proud of your bake shop."

An uneasiness settled in Nina's stomach. The woman's praise wasn't a casual compliment. There was a calculated gleam in Katherine's eyes, a purpose that put Nina on guard.

She turned to face the woman as the smell of coffee filled the air. "What exactly can I do for you, Ms. Brothers?"

"Cards on the table?"

"Please." Nina folded her arms over her chest and leaned against the counter.

"I'd like to buy your bakery."

Nina stared at the elegant creature and blinked. "You want to what?"

"Buy your bakery." The woman's tone was straightforward as if she hadn't just dropped a bombshell. "I knew it was exactly the place I'd been looking for when I tasted those amazing madeleines. It's right here in the town square, in the heart of Kringle. It's got charm, it's got history, it's got *je ne sais quoi*."

"S-sell the bakery?" Nina's brain hung in neutral, barely able to process what the woman was saying.

Katherine Brothers nodded long and slow, putting extra emphasis on her intent. "Yes."

Nina shook her head. "My grandparents started this bakery, and then my parents took over and now they've passed it on to me. It's been in our family for three generations."

"Yes." Nod, nod, nod. Seriously, the woman was a bobblehead. "That's what makes it *so* special. That and your amazing cookies."

"The bakery isn't for sale."

Katherine narrowed her eyes and deepened her smile. "Oh, sweetheart, *everything* is for sale for the right price."

Goosebumps skittered up Nina's arms. So many times, she wished to be free of the bakery. She'd never really had a choice of career because of her family legacy. She'd gotten her degree in business with the sole purpose of eventually taking over the bakery from her parents and it happened faster than she'd intended when her father's rheumatoid arthritis forced him and her mother to move to a drier climate. Nina had never worked anywhere besides the bakery.

"Here's what I'm prepared to offer..." Then Katherine Brothers named a number so high Nina was certain she heard incorrectly.

"Excuse me?" She blinked.

Katherine repeated herself.

"I-I don't know what to say."

Katherine pulled a glossy business card from her designer purse and handed it to Nina. "I'd like to keep you on as manager. Name your salary. You wouldn't have to worry about anything—you'd still be running the place but with financial backing and resources to expand and hire someone to help you."

Nina took the card. The name and logo blurred before her eyes. This was a dream offer. She would never get another one like it.

"Just think about it. Take all the time you need. I know this is a busy time of year."

The door opened, bell jingling, and one of her regulars, Mrs. Claiborne, walked in. "Mornin', Nina. I need two boxes of donuts for the angel tree volunteers."

"Coming right up," Nina said, turning toward her customer. "All honey glazed, or do you want some chocolate?"

"A box of each." Mrs. Claiborne eyed Ms. Brothers, then turned her attention back to Nina. "You're still coming to help set up for the pageant on Thursday afternoon, right? And the potluck afterward?"

"Absolutely." Nina boxed up the donuts.

Katherine Brothers cleared her throat. "Just give me a call when you're ready, Ms. Ellis. I'll be waiting." With a wave of her hand, she strolled out and set the bell jingling again.

"Who was that?" Mrs. Claiborne asked, staring after the elegant woman.

"You saw her too?" Nina asked, clutching the business card. "I was beginning to think I imagined her."

Garrett Ellis watched Jean Deerling lay down her last domino to a chorus of groans and laughter from the table. She had a way of making winning look effortless, always one step ahead of everyone else.

"The tournament is mine!" she said and rubbed her palms together as the organizer declared her the winner and gave her the gift certificate to a four-day stay for two on Padre Island.

He wasn't surprised. Jean was sharp, with a quick mind and quicker wit. She didn't miss much. He'd lost out of the tournament in the previous round and had been watching the few competitors left at the table, secretly rooting for Jean to win over the men.

From his spot across the room, he noticed the way her eyes darted around, taking in the women who had been circling him like hawks all afternoon. He suppressed a smile, sipping his coffee and leaning back in his chair.

It was the annual Kringle Senior Citizen Community Center Christmas party, and everyone was in a particularly festive mood, probably because his friend Charlie Gunter had spiked the punch bowl.

Jean stood up, her gaze fixed on him, and he

felt his heart beat a little faster. She was a striking woman, confident in a way that drew people to her. He'd always thought of her as more of an acquaintance, but lately, he'd noticed the way she looked at him, and it stirred something he hadn't felt in a long time.

As she made her way over, Garrett saw a couple of the other women shift, their gazes narrowing slightly. He couldn't help but be impressed. Jean was bold, that was for sure, and she looked radiant in pine-green slacks and a red cashmere sweater.

She slipped between the tables, weaving past a tray of barbecue sliders and a platter of cookies from Ellis Early Eats frosted in red and green.

"I'm gonna get some more punch," Charlie said. "You want some?"

"No, I'm good," Garrett said, his eyes locked on Jean.

Charlie winked and nudged him in the elbow and then ambled off to the beverage table.

"Hello, Garrett," Jean said.

"Jean." He nodded and took a casual sip of his coffee. "Congrats on besting those old codgers. You'll have fun on Padre."

"Sadly," Jean said, lowering her lashes. "I have

no one to accompany me on the trip, but then again, I've never been afraid to travel solo."

Was that an invitation? Garrett's heart skipped a couple of beats. Maybe he should lay off the coffee.

"Enjoying the party?" he asked because he didn't know what else to say.

"It's a little stuffy in here. Would you mind accompanying me outside for a walk?" She put a hand on his forearm.

"Sure." He tossed the paper cup in the nearby trash can, wondering what brought all this on, but not wanting to jinx things by asking.

Jean slipped her arm through his and leaned in to whisper, "I saw Betty Pats heading your way and thought you might need a rescue."

"Oh," he said, feeling a little disappointed. "Is that what this is?"

"I know how she can natter on, bless her heart."

"A rescue, huh?" He lifted his eyebrows and quirked a grin.

"Let's call it that, just in case."

"All right, then." He guided her to the coatrack. "Which one is yours?"

"The red one."

Of course, it was. Nothing shy and retiring about Jean. He helped her on with her coat, then held open the door. They stepped outside together.

"Which direction?" he asked.

"How about the lake?"

"That's a good mile away."

"Are your knees acting up?"

"No."

"Mine either."

"It's another mile back."

"I'm fully aware of how walking works, Garrett Ellis."

He laughed and they set off, the fallen leaves crunching beneath their feet, the afternoon sun peeking through the clouds.

"We should do this more often," she said. "Why haven't we done it before?"

"I don't know." He slid a glance over at her, her arm still tucked through his. It felt nice against his side.

Jean smiled, pleasure in her eyes. "Are you planning on attending the Danvers Christmas Eve party at the Double D?"

"I go every year they have the event," he said. "I delivered both Ryan and Jenny."

"You delivered most everyone in Kringle."

"Not your kids." He'd been the only doctor in Kringle for years, but Jean had never come to see him, preferring to drive to Fort Worth instead, but he'd never taken it personally.

"It's nice to see the Danvers' place return to life," she said. "I was afraid Ryan and Jenny weren't ever going to shake their grief."

"Me too. It's a hard thing, for sure. Losing people you love. The pain never really goes away, does it?" Garrett gazed out over Lake Kringle and watched a pair of cranes skim over the water.

Jean gave his arm a gentle squeeze. "No, it doesn't, but we're still here, Garrett. We're still living."

"True."

"How's bakery life treating you?"

"It's a lot sweeter than medicine," he deadpanned.

Jean pulled back and stopped walking.

He stopped, too. "What is it?"

"You're a funny man, Garrett Ellis. Why didn't I know that about you?"

"Probably because we've never spent much time getting to know each other. All these years, we've been mere acquaintances because you didn't trust my medical opinion," he teased.

"Oh, but that is not true," she said. "I just wanted to keep my secrets secret."

"What secrets might those be?"

"Well, would it be as much fun to walk with me if you were thinking about that ugly scar on my knee? Or how hideous my appendix looked when it came out?"

He laughed. "So you're an enigma."

"It makes this a lot more fun, don't you think?"

"Walking? Or did you have something else in mind?"

"I might," she said. "If you're interested. I did win a trip for two to Padre."

"Why don't you come by the bakery on Thursday morning, say around seven, if you're an early riser? We can have a cup of coffee and some of Nina's blueberry cinnamon rolls and a good conversation to start the day, see how things go."

"Call it date?"

"Yes, Jean, I think we should."

CHAPTER 6

CURLED up on the couch in her Stanton Street cottage, Nina stared at the Christmas tree winking at her from across the room. The mantel clock ticked, keeping time with wood crackling in the fireplace.

Sell the bakery? A novel thought. Scary and yet... provocative.

Nina fingered Katherine Brothers' card and bit her bottom lip.

For the past two hours, she mulled over the extravagant offer. She tried to distract herself with Dicken's *A Christmas Carol* and then a cup of chamomile tea and madeleine cookies. A comfy fleece reindeer-themed throw and her sweet calico Speckles did little to calm her restless thoughts.

The kind of money Katherine Brothers flaunted would change *everything*, and that was the problem. Nina wasn't ready for change.

With a sigh, she got up and walked to the window. She pushed aside the lace curtains and peered out at her quiet neighborhood. Festive Christmas lights hung from the houses, and candles flickered in windows. The holiday cheer should have lifted her spirits but only highlighted her loneliness.

She closed her eyes and rested her forehead against the cool glass. What would Gee say about the offer? Would he want her to sell out? Forbid it? Or tell her the decision was up to her?

Whatever his reaction, if she told him of the offer it was bound to stir memories of her grandmother. The bakery had been Ellie's pride and joy. Her grandmother poured heart and soul into her breads and pastries. The family had just been along for the ride, and then once Ellie was gone, they continued on to keep her alive in spirit. Every corner of the bakery, every original recipe, held memories and letting go of that felt like losing her all over again.

But the idea of not waking up at dawn every day, of not constantly worrying about keeping a struggling business afloat... well, the money Katherine Brothers offered was life changing and if Nina stayed on to manage the shop, she could hire people to arrive at 3 a.m. to start the baking.

What would life be like without that weight, without those expectations? What would the freedom to find her own path feel like?

She plopped back onto the couch, Katherine's card still in her hand. How could she sell? Gee wouldn't express his hurt to hurt, but the bakery was all that remained of her grandmother, of the life he shared with Ellie. Of course, he wouldn't want her to sell.

And yet, Gee would never stand in Nina's way. He'd tell her to do what she thought was best. She couldn't bear his kind understanding, his sacrifice.

Nina picked up her phone and wrote a text.

> Thank you for the offer, Ms. Brothers, but we're not interested in selling.

She stared at the words for a moment, and then she hit 'send.'

With less than two weeks before Christmas Eve, Ryan had tackled his party to-do list every evening after he finished his ranching chores. Thanks to vendors like Nina, the photographer, Ava Sutton, and the party supplier offering him either discounts or payment plans, he was back under budget.

But just barely.

On Wednesday night, he cleaned out the barn, which, in between holiday celebrations, served as a storage unit. He owned a second, newer barn for the livestock. Stacks of crates, boxes and containers needed to moving into the spare bedroom until after the event. Luckily, he and Jenny labeled and organized everything, so it was simply a matter of toting things from one place to the other.

For the past two hours he shifted and moved boxes, but his mind wasn't on the work. His thoughts kept drifting back to Nina and the dance they shared in her bakery.

He thought of how they laughed together as he twirled her around, the softness of her hand in his. He hadn't expected to feel anything special, let alone the strange lightness that lingered long after they stopped dancing.

He reached for a dusty, square tin hidden high

on a shelf, and recognized it instantly. His mother's treasured recipe box that she once kept in a prominent place on the kitchen counter tucked next to the flour jar.

Ryan opened the lid, the smell of aged paper and cinnamon rising to meet him. Inside, the recipe cards were yellowed with age, and the handwriting familiar and flowery. He flipped through them, his fingers brushing over titles that brought back snippets of long-ago holidays.

His pulse quickened as memories flooded his mind. Mom's head thrown back laughing, flour on the end of her nose. Dad waltzing Mom around the kitchen to "I Saw Mommy Kissing Santa Claus." Ryan and Jenny sitting on the stairs on Christmas morning, giggling together and waiting for the signal to come down and open their presents.

With each recipe, another memory.

Then his fingers hit one labeled *Heavenly Honey Buns,* the ink slightly smudged, as if the card got wet at some point. Ryan stopped and plucked it from the box.

Those honey buns were his absolute favorite— soft, sweet, and filled with the flavor of home. After their mother died, he'd told Jenny not to make them, the thought of tasting them again too sharp, too close to the bone.

He hadn't thought about the heavenly honey buns in years. Had almost forgotten how much they once meant to him.

Almost.

Ryan set the card down, the instructions staring back at him. The recipe felt like a challenge, like something left unfinished.

Should he make them for the church potluck tomorrow night?

Could he?

He bit down on his bottom lip, sorrow bitter on his tongue.

And then the bitterness swept away as his mouth filled with yeast and honey, tastier than any cinnamon roll. He saw the domed bee-hive-shaped buns with the sweet caramelized surface his mother molded by hand. Her supreme recipe was nothing like those gummy prepacked things in the store. Mom's honey buns were a thing of glory.

Did Nina ever make honey buns? Ryan couldn't recall seeing them in her bakery, but he was certain she knew how. She was a talented baker.

He read over the recipe. It sounded pretty

complicated, but he'd watched his mom make the pastries dozens of times. If he messed up, he'd just try again.

Do you really want to stir this all up again?

Ryan blew out his breath. Did he?

To be honest? He didn't know. Mostly, he compartmentalize his emotions from the party, but the thought of sharing his mother's prized recipe with the community, with the people who remembered her, felt like something he needed to do.

For Mom.

And for himself.

He stood for a long moment in the silent barn, the darkness outside surrounding him, the old recipe card in his hand, a spark of hope in his heart. The potluck was nothing really, an everyday gathering, but somehow, it seemed more significant than that, like a chance to bring something back to life.

Ryan didn't know whether the honey buns would taste the same or even if he could get through it without breaking down, but maybe that was the point. Perhaps it wasn't about recreating what was lost but about finding what remained.

About creating something new in the process.

He closed the recipe box, keeping out the

Heavenly Honey Buns index card, shut up the barn and called it a night.

And when he fell asleep, he dreamed of honey buns and waltzing under the mistletoe with Nina Ellis.

———

Excitement loomed like a wooly bear in Garrett's imagination, big and scary. Last night, just before he fell asleep, Jean Deerling texted that she was looking forward to their morning coffee date.

The operative word being *date*.

He hadn't dated since he'd lost Ellie. Hadn't even had the desire. But now, he wanted to see Jean. Oh yes, he did, but was this old dog too tired to hunt? At seventy-six, he still had a few good years left in him, but not all that many.

It was still dark out when unlocked the front door and stepped into the bakery, the familiar scent of yeast and cinnamon calming his nerves. It was just coffee with Jean. No need for his heart to be hammering like a teenager's, right?

"Gee?" Nina called from the kitchen. "That you?"

"Yeah, it's me. Thought I'd come in early today and help you open up."

Nina appeared in the doorway, flour dusting her apron, her hair escaping from her messy bun. "Well, well, don't you look dapper this morning?"

Garrett's neck burned, and he smoothed a hand over the flannel shirt, still creased from the packaging. "Nothing special."

"New shirt, starched jeans. What's up?" Her smile teased.

"Can't a man make an effort without the third degree?"

Nina laughed. "Oh, Gee, you're as transparent as cellophane. What's her name?"

"I'm having coffee with Jean Deerling, but don't make a thing of it, okay?"

Nina held up her palms. "Far be it from me to stand in the way of Cupid's arrow."

Garrett cleared his throat. "What can I do to help?"

Nina plucked a piece of chalk from the black-board. "Fill out the specials."

"Which is?"

"BLT and potato soup for lunch. Chocolate profiteroles, pecan pie and pumpkin bread are the desserts of the day."

"On it." Garrett pulled out the step stool they kept under the counter and climbed up to erase the previous day's specials to write in the new additions. He really enjoyed this second act with his granddaughter after retiring from medicine. Helping out in the bakery was a way to stay busy and connected with the community he loved so much, but lately, he'd felt... well... *bored.*

He needed something new in his life. A challenge, perhaps, or an adventure. Could that be Jean?

Part of him felt torn. He'd loved Ellie with everything inside him, and they'd been a good match, a solid team, but she'd been gone for over a decade. He missed her. Missed being in a loving relationship.

He wanted to love again, but he was scared to hope. Afraid to try. What if it didn't work out?

Oh, but what if it did?

It was Ellie's voice in his head, optimistic and encouraging. She'd told him when she was sick that she wanted him to marry again, to move on, embrace life, but he'd been reluctant. Worried that no one, nothing, could ever measure up to what they had. It wouldn't be the same.

It doesn't need to be the same, silly goose. It

shouldn't be the same. It'll be a new love. A new way of being.

Shaking off the memories, Garrett found ways to be helpful, keeping himself busy until seven—polishing the counter, greeting customers, filling orders, and ringing up purchases.

The bell jingled at 6:59. He raised his head, and his gaze landed on Jean as she came through the door.

His heart skipped a beat.

She looked him straight in the eyes and smiled, resplendent in a deep green sweater, which compliments her silver hair, black car coat and matching black slacks. "Good morning, Garrett."

"Morning, Jean." A rush of heat fled up his throat, and he felt ridiculously out of his element. "You look fantastic."

Jean's smile deepened. "Thank you. You're looking quite snazzy yourself."

Nina cleared her throat.

Garrett looked over to see his granddaughter gazing at him with affection. "Why don't you two have a seat? I'll bring over some coffee and some crullers. They're fresh out of the fryer."

"That sounds lovely," Jean said.

"How do you take your coffee?" Nina asked her.

Jean gazed into Garrett's eyes. "Black with three sugars. I like it strong but sweet."

Garrett stuck out a hand to usher Jean over to a table in the far corner. He pulled out the chair for her and cast a glance toward Nina who had an absent-minded look in her eyes and slight frown tugged at her lips as she poured up the coffee.

Something was bothering her. Garrett knew his granddaughter well since they'd worked closely together for the past four years, and he could tell when something was eating at her. Was it Jean? Was she bothered that he had a date?

"Penny for your thoughts?" Jean said, drawing his attention back to her.

Garrett sighed, debating how much to share as sat down across from her. "It's probably nothing, but... I'm a bit worried about Nina. She seems... off somehow for the last couple of days."

"In what way?"

"I'm not sure exactly. Just a feeling, I suppose. Like she's carrying some kind of burden, she doesn't feel comfortable sharing with me."

Jean reached across the table, taking his hand. "Have you asked her about it?"

"Not yet. I don't want to pry."

Jean nodded. "I get that. Sometimes, it's difficult to know when we're helping or interfering with family."

"I worry that she's working too hard. Not getting a chance to have a life of her own. I can't help feeling like she got saddled with the bakery, and she feels compelled to keep it up out of tradition. I don't want her to feel obligated—" Garrett broke off as Nina came over with the coffee and crullers.

"Enjoy!" She gave them a warm smile, but beneath it, Garrett spied shadows under her eyes as if she hadn't slept well.

"Nina are you okay?" he asked.

Her smile wavered, but just for a moment. "Of course, Gee. Why wouldn't it be?"

The bell chimed, and Nina hurried off to greet the new customers.

Jean touched his hand, and he turned back to her. "Trust her to tell you in her own time if something is bothering her."

Garrett nodded. "You're right. I know you're right. It's... well..."

"You love her and want to protect her."

He nodded. "I do."

"Perhaps she feels the same about you." Jean peered at him over the rim of her coffee mug.

Whatever secret Nina was keeping, he wouldn't push. Jean was right. He needed to give his granddaughter space.

"Oh my gosh," Jean said, biting into her cruller. "This is delicious!"

"After breakfast, would you like to go to the Farmer's Market?" he invited.

"Why, Garrett, I would love that."

They made small talk, discussing their Christmas plans and finished their crullers. Then Garrett got up to make them to-go coffees as Jean shrugged into her coat. He caught Nina's eye as she turned to get pastries for a customer from the display case.

She raised an eyebrow, glancing from him to Jean.

Garrett gave a half-shrug and a smile.

His granddaughter smiled back and then returned her attention to the customer. He would talk to Nina later about whatever was weighing on her, about the future of the bakery, and about the delicate balance between independence and family.

CHAPTER 7

RYAN HALTED at the threshold of the church, his mother's recipe of Heavenly Honey Buns clutched in his hands. They turned out delicious. The best ever.

Swallowing hard, he pushed open the door and stepped inside.

The fragrance of incense and beeswax candles washed over him, intertwined with the muted strains of "Silent Night" drifting in from the fellowship hall.

A memory floated through him—his mother directing the children's choir, his father helping to set up the nativity scene.

He blinked hard, willing away the sting in his eyes. The fellowship hall bustled with activity.

Folding chairs scraped against the worn linoleum as volunteers arranged them for the potluck. Cardboard boxes overflowed with tinsel and ornaments, their contents spilling onto tables and chairs. In the auditorium, near the stage, a tall Fraser fir stood sentinel, its branches bare and waiting.

Ryan's gaze swept the room, cataloging the changes over the years from when his parents were alive. New curtains framed the windows, their deep blue a stark contrast to the faded yellow. The walls bore a fresh coat of paint, hiding the scuff marks and fingerprints of years past.

But beneath the surface updates, the bones of the place remained unchanged. The identical wooden beams crossed the ceiling. The same stained-glass windows filtered the late afternoon sunlight into pools of color on the floor.

He took a steadying breath, his fingers clutching the pan of honey buns. The familiar ache in his chest—a constant companion since his parents' passing—intensified. He was here to help, to fulfill a promise to Mrs. Claiborne. Nothing more. Get in, do the work, get out. Simple.

But as his eyes adjusted to the glow of the hall, movement near the stage caught his attention.

Dark hair, gleaming under the lights. A laugh, bright and clear, cut through the din.

Nina.

Ryan's pulse quickened, a staccato rhythm against his rib cage.

She stood with her grandfather, Dr. Ellis, her hands moving animatedly as she spoke. Even from across the room, he absorbed her energy. She fit here, among the tinsel and poinsettias, as if she'd stepped out of one of Ryan's memories and into the present.

He hadn't expected her to be here. Hadn't prepared himself for how seeing her affected him. Their dance in her bakery's kitchen was still fresh in his mind—the feel of her hand in his, the scent of vanilla clinging to her hair, the way the world had narrowed to just the two of them.

For a heartbeat, Ryan considered retreat. He could slip away unnoticed. Make up some excuse about the ranch needing his attention, but even as the thought formed, he dismissed it. Mrs. Claiborne was counting on him and running from his feelings—well, he'd done enough of that over the years.

He moved forward and the floorboards creaked beneath his boots. He headed to the kitchenette, where people settled the dishes they'd brought onto the long communal table and he set his honey buns down at the dessert section with pies, cakes, and cookies. He murmured greetings to people and engaged in chitchat, but even when he wasn't looking at her, Ryan was acutely aware of Nina.

His legs seemed to have a mind of their own, drawing him from the dining hall and into the auditorium.

Nina turned. Her gaze swept past him, then snapped back, recognition dawning, her eyes widening in surprise.

Ryan nodded in greeting, aiming for casual and missing by a mile. He was aware of every step, every breath. The memory of their dance hovered between them, unspoken but impossible to ignore.

"Ryan!" Mrs. Claiborne's voice cut through his thoughts. She bustled toward him, arms laden with garlands that shed tinsel with each step. "You made it! We've got quite the to-do list, and I'm tickled you're here to help."

He pulled a palm down his mouth. "Happy to pitch in. What needs doing?"

Mrs. Claiborne's eyes twinkled, a knowing look that made Ryan want to squirm. "Well, now that you mention it—" She gestured at a large figure propped against the far wall. "We've got ourselves quite the celestial being this year. Think you can lend a hand getting her airborne?"

The angel was enormous, easily five feet tall, with a wingspan that threatened to overtake half the stage. The angel's face tilted slightly downward and wore an expression of serene benevolence that seemed at odds with its imposing size.

"Where do you need her hung?" he asked.

Mrs. Claiborne pointed to two chains hanging from the ceiling just above the stage. Tricky sure, but manageable.

"Sure," Ryan said. "I can manage that."

Mrs. Claiborne beamed. "Wonderful! Nina will be your partner in this heavenly endeavor. It's a two-person job, that's for certain."

Of course it was.

Ryan flicked a look at Nina, who met his gaze with an unreadable expression. Her lips quirked in a tentative smile that didn't quite reach her eyes, and his heart backflipped.

"Right," he said, rubbing the taut muscles at his nape. "Let's get to it, then."

"How do you want to handle this?" Nina tucked a lock of hair behind her ear and shot him a sidelong glance.

Ryan eyed the angel. "Let's see how much she weighs."

Nina circled the angle. "She's papier-mâché, so not too heavy, I'm guessing. Just an awkward shape. Mrs. Claiborne said the angel is new this year, donated by Chloe and Evan Connor. Apparently, Mrs. C didn't realize how big it was until it arrived."

Ryan ran a hand along the angel's base, feeling for any handholds. The surface was smooth, except for the small rings on either end that would attach to the chains, offering little in the way of grip. "How did they even get it in here?"

"Two deacons and a dolly," Nina gave a wry smile. "Which we don't have the luxury of right now."

They stood for a moment, considering the logistical challenge before them. The ladder waited several yards away, and between it and the angel stood a maze of chairs, boxes, and bustling volunteers.

Ryan squatted down, examining the angel's base. "Okay, I think if I take the bottom and you guide the top, we should make short work of this."

Nina positioned herself at the angel's head, her

hands hovering uncertainly over the angel's wings and shoulders. "Ready when you are."

With a grunt, Ryan heaved upward, lifting the base of the angel. The weight was more substantial than he'd anticipated for papier-mâché, and he put extra muscle into it.

"Got it?" Nina asked as she steadied the upper portion.

Ryan adjusted his grip and nodded. The angel swayed precariously between them, its wings brushing against nearby decorations. "Alright, let's move."

They began their slow procession across the fellowship hall, the angel swaying between them. Ryan walked backward, relying on Nina's guidance to navigate the obstacle course of holiday preparations.

"Left a bit," Nina said. "Watch out for the box of ornaments behind you."

Ryan sidestepped, feeling the burning in his arms intensify. Sweat beaded on his forehead despite the cool air of the church but he refused to waver.

They were halfway to the ladder when the angel's wing caught on a string of lights draped over a nearby table. The sudden resistance caused Ryan to stumble and nearly lose his grip.

"Whoa!" Nina leaned forward to steady the angel and her sudden movement brought her face inches from Ryan's, their noses almost touching over the angel's shoulder.

For a heartbeat, they froze, eyes locked.

Ryan saw flecks of gold in Nina's brown irises and felt her heated breath on his cheek. The weight of the angel seemed to disappear, replaced by the overwhelming awareness of Nina.

A crash from across the room broke the moment. They startled, nearly dropping the angel.

"Everything okay over there?" Mrs. Claiborne called from somewhere behind them.

"Fine!" Nina said, her voice higher than usual. "Just a minor detour."

Another few yards zigzagging around impediments and they finally reached the ladder. The hard part was yet to come, but at least now Ryan had something to focus on besides the way Nina electrified the air around him.

"Okay," he said, setting his end of the angel down. "How do we get this thing up there?"

Nina bit her lip, considering the challenge. "I think I'll have to go up first, and you'll boost her up to me. Unless you want to try lifting Miss Angel over your head?"

Ryan glanced at the ladder, then back at the ornament, mentally calculating angles and weight distribution. "No, you're right. It'll have to be a handoff. But Nina..." He met her eyes. "Be careful up there. This thing's unwieldy, and I don't want you falling."

A soft smile played at the corners of Nina's mouth. "Don't worry. I'm tougher than I look. Besides," she added, a hint of teasing in her voice, "I know you'll catch me if I fall."

"I'll do my best to keep us both grounded." Ryan aimed for levity, but his voice came out deep and a little shaky. His gaze dropped to her lips before he could stop himself, remembering how close they'd been during their dance.

He held the angel steady while she scampered up the ladder with ease, her movements fluid and assured.

It struck Ryan how at home she seemed—not just in the church, but in her own skin. He admired her grace and poise. How was it he hadn't noticed her before? Had he really been that entrenched in grief?

Nina reached the top rung. "Okay, pass her up."

Ryan tilted back his head and eyed her. "You sure you can handle it?"

She made "gimme" motions.

Reluctantly, he grasped the base of the angel and lifted it up, waiting until she had a solid grasp on the angel's head before he raised it higher.

Her balance wavered.

Alarm dashed through him. "You okay?"

"I'm good. Keep 'er coming."

Every muscle in his body coiled, ready to spring into action at the slightest sign of trouble. He widened his stance and pushed a bit more of the angel upward toward her. Dang it, he should be on the ladder, not her.

"Almost... there," Nina murmured and pulled the unwieldy angel high enough for him to rest the angel's base on the step below her.

"You got it?" he asked, reluctant to let go.

"Uh-huh."

Two eyebolts with chains and latchets dangled down from the ceiling, awaiting the regal heavenly presence.

Nina tucked the angel's head under her arm and stretched forward toward the high ceiling, reaching for the first hook. The movement caused her sweater to ride up, exposing a sliver of skin above the waistband of her jeans.

Ryan's mouth went dry. He had a wild urge to press his lips in that sweet spot. *Stop it, Danvers. Don't get distracted.*

"Careful," he said.

"I've got it." She secured the hook at the angel's crown to the first chain latch. "I just need to—*ayeee!*"

Her foot slipped.

One moment, Nina stood perched atop the ladder, the next, she was falling, the angel swinging by her head, body free-floating through the air.

Time slowed.

Ryan saw every detail with crystal clarity—the widening of Nina's eyes, the way her hair fanned out around her face, the gasp that escaped her glossy pink lips.

"Nina!" Ryan lunged forward, arms outstretched.

Nina collided with his chest, and he folded his arms around her even as the impact knocked the wind from his lungs and sent him stumbling backward. He dug in his heels to keep from toppling over.

But gravity won.

Ryan tumbled onto his butt, taking Nina with him.

For a heartbeat, the world narrowed to just the two of them. Nina's face inches from his, her breath coming in short, rapid bursts. Her hands clutched at his shoulders, fingers digging into the fabric of his shirt. He could feel the fast thud of her heart against his chest, matching the frantic pace of his own.

The scent of her surrounded him—vanilla and cinnamon and something uniquely Nina. It transported him back to her bakery, to the moment when the lines between friendship and something more started to blur.

"Ryan?" she whispered. "Are you okay?"

"Yes," he said, his voice coming out far softer than he intended. "Are you?"

He was acutely aware of every point of contact between them—her hands on his shoulders, his arms around her waist, the press of her body against his.

Nina nodded, but her gaze remained fixed on his, wide and startled. "Yeah, I'm fine. Thanks to you."

"Good." He knew he should let go, get up, and

make sure she was steady on her feet, but his arms seemed to have a mind of their own, holding her close. His fingers splayed against the small of her back, feeling the warmth of her skin through the material of her sweater.

Nina's breath hitched.

A slight sound that sent a shiver down Ryan's spine. Her gaze dropped to his lips for a fraction of a second before darting back up to meet his eyes. The air between them crackled with unspoken tension, with possibilities neither of them dared voice.

If a roomful of volunteers hadn't rushed over, Ryan had no idea what might have happened. He might have kissed her, or she might have kissed him, or they might have equally consumed each other.

But instead, people pulled them to their feet, clucking and cooing over their mishap. Nina stepped back, pushing her hair from her face. Her cheeks flushed a rosy hue that spread down her neck and disappeared beneath the collar of her sweater.

"Thank you again," she said. "For catching me."

Ryan let his arms flop to his sides, immediately

missing her. "Anytime, though maybe we should look into some non-falling-related activities."

A small laugh escaped Nina, genuine despite its shakiness. "Probably a good idea. I'm not sure my heart can take much more excitement."

Mrs. Claiborne hustled over. "Oh my stars! Nina, dear, are you all right? That was quite the tumble!"

"I'm fine, Mrs. Claiborne. Ryan's quick reflexes saved the day... and me."

Mrs. Claiborne's gaze flicked between Nina and Ryan with a shrewd expression that made him want to fidget. "Well, thank goodness for that." She patted Ryan's shoulder. "You've always been a quick one, haven't you? Always there when someone needs a helping hand."

Ryan shifted, hyperaware of Nina beside him. "Just happened to be in the right place. Now, I better get that angel secured before she falls on someone."

Turning, he scaled the ladder and attached the angel's back half to the second chain latch and when he glanced down, he saw Mrs. Claiborne escorting Nina to the kitchen.

And Nina was looking back at him.

CHAPTER 8

NINA SAT at one of the long folding tables in the fellowship hall, her plate filled with green bean casserole, sweet potatoes, and a slice of ham. The aroma of all the homemade dishes filled the air and mixed with the animated conversation.

People laughed, joked, discussed tomorrow's upcoming pageant, and complimented each other's food dishes. Kids darted between the tables, playing tag, and giggling. Every so often, someone shouted at them to settle down while the faint strains of Christmas carols played in the background.

Nina poked at her food, her mind miles away from the homey gathering. No matter how hard she tried to focus on the conversation around her, she couldn't stop thinking about what had happened on the ladder just a short time ago.

The sensation of falling—her heart in her throat, the weightlessness as the ladder tipped still fresh in her mind. Then the solid feel of Ryan's arms catching her, the way his strong body steadied her as if he knew exactly what she needed.

It shook her more than she cared to admit.

Across the table, Gee watched her, his eyes dark with concern. "You sure you're okay after that little mishap earlier? You've been staring at that green bean casserole like it's gonna jump off your plate and eat *you*."

Nina met his gaze. "I'm fine, Gee. Just wool-gathering, I guess."

Jean Deerling, seated beside her grandfather, reached across the table and gave Nina's hand a gentle pat. "That was quite a tumble, Nina. You had us all worried for a second there. Good thing Ryan was quick on his feet."

"Yeah, he... he caught me. I'm lucky he was there."

Gee nodded. "Between the bakery, the holiday rush, and helping out here at the church, you're running yourself ragged."

"'Tis the season," she said with a laugh,

brushing off his fretting. She had been stretched thin and today's fall had made her realize how distracted she'd been, especially when it came to Ryan Danvers.

"I'm sorry your folks won't be with us for Christmas," Jean said. "Garrett was just telling me they were spending the holiday with your mom's sister in Flagstaff."

"Yes," Nina said, feeling a tug of loneliness. "But they'll be here for New Year's and we'll exchange gifts then."

"You and Garrett are welcome to join our boisterous bunch for Christmas Day," Jean invited. "We're having tamales and enchiladas."

"Thank you for the invitation." Nina nodded. "Hopefully we can make it." She didn't want to commit in case something happened with Ryan.

Pipe dreaming, much?

Mrs. Claiborne bustled by with a platter of deviled eggs. She paused beside Nina. "That angel sure looks beautiful up there. You and Ryan did a fine job. Just don't go scaring us again, Nina. I about had a heart attack when you fell."

"I'll try my best," Nina said, her face heating again, but this time, it was from more than just the fall. It was the memory of being in Ryan's arms, the way his touch had sent a jolt through her that she wasn't entirely ready for.

Gee set down his fork. "I'm going for those honey buns I saw on the dessert table. Anyone else want one?"

"I heard Ryan made those," Jean said. "It's his mom's recipe. Bring me one, too, , unless you want to split one. They're huge."

"Splitting it is." Her grandfather got up and headed for the desserts.

Nina blinked at Jean, her fork freezing in midair. "Ryan baked?"

Her eyes darted to the dessert table where the honey buns sat, golden brown and inviting, nestled between Jean's pecan pie and Sarah Porter's famous fruit salad.

Jean grinned. "You wouldn't expect a man like him to bake, but I guess he's full of surprises."

Nina's pulse quickened. Ryan, baking? That was unexpected.

"You gotta wonder why some woman hasn't locked that man down by now," Jean said, sipping her iced tea.

Indeed. Why *wasn't* he married?

Nina arose from her seat. "I think I'll take a spin around the dessert table myself."

Weaving through the crowded fellowship hall, Nina searched for Ryan. He stood near the coffee station, chatting with a few of the older men from the church and her stomach somersaulted. She willed him to look her way, but he didn't.

Disappointed, she wandered to the dessert table, picked up a honey bun with tongs and settled it onto her plate. She took a bite, savoring the sweet flavor. It melted in her mouth. Perfection. She couldn't have baked a better honey bun herself.

She closed her eyes and took another bite. "Mmm."

"So, what do you think?"

She turned, startled to find Ryan standing right next to her, his eyes fixed on the honey bun in her hand. She swallowed quickly, the taste lingering on her tongue. "They're... incredible. I didn't know you could bake."

"Me either, to be honest." He shrugged and smiled. "It was my mom's recipe. She used to make them every Christmas." He glanced toward the table where Gee sat with Jean. "Figured it was time to bring it back."

Nina looked down at the honey bun, then back up at him. "That's really special. Your mother would be proud of these and of you for keeping her tradition alive."

Ryan gave a quiet nod, but she could see the flicker of something in his eyes—grief, maybe, or the weight of memories. "It's a small thing, but it helped to remember her, you know?"

"I do know," she said, thinking of her grandmother Ellie and her love for the bakery. Immediately, she felt guilty for the few moments she'd considered selling the bakery to Katherine Brothers.

Ryan's tender smile touched her heart. She had always known Ryan as the quiet, dependable rancher, but today—first with the ladder, and now with these honey buns—he was showing her sides of himself she'd never seen before.

And she wasn't sure what to do with that.

"Well, I better get back to Gee," she said.

"Uh-huh." Ryan nodded.

"See you later," she said and went back to her seat.

"Well, well," Gee said, a mischievous glint in his eye. "Looks like you two were having quite the conversation over there."

"We were just talking about the honey buns, Gee. Nothing more."

Jean leaned in, her voice low and conspiratorial. "Oh, I don't know about that. I saw the way he was looking at you, Nina. That boy's got stars in his eyes."

"Jean!" Nina said, glancing around to make sure no one had overheard. "It's not like that. We're just... friends."

But even as she said it, Nina felt a flutter in her stomach. The memory of Ryan's smile, warm and genuine, flashed through her mind.

Could she actually get her Christmas wish?

Her gaze drifted back to Ryan. He'd moved to a table near the window, and he was deep in conversation with his brother-in-law, Scott Finley, and a few other local men. The overhead lighting caught his profile and showcased his strong jawline.

He looked up and caught her staring. He gave her a slight nod, the corner of his mouth quirking up in a half smile.

She quickly looked away, her heart racing.

"Nina?" Jean's voice cut through her thoughts. "Are you sure you're feeling alright? Your cheeks are flushed. The flu's been going around."

Nina forced a smile. "I'm fine, really. Just... thinking about everything I need to do at the bakery tomorrow and speaking of, I really need to get going. My bedtime is fast approaching."

After bidding her grandfather and Jean good night, she gathered her things and headed for the door just as Ryan was walking out.

They almost collided.

"Sorry," they said in unison, then laughed.

"Great minds think alike," Ryan said with a grin.

"Two early risers knowing when to call it a night," she said.

"May I walk you to your car?" he asked.

"I would appreciate that."

He held the door open for her to go first. Outside, the crisp night air nipped at Nina's cheeks. Ryan fell into step beside her, his presence comforting on the cool December evening. They didn't speak, but it wasn't awkward. In fact, it was nice not needing to say anything.

They reached her car, and Nina fumbled with her keys, suddenly reluctant for the evening to end. As she opened the door, she turned back to Ryan.

"Nina?" Ryan said.

"Yes?"

He cleared his throat. "I was wondering if

you'd like to go to the Kringle Christmas Tree
Lighting with me this Saturday. The usual carolers
will be there, and I heard there might even be a
horse-drawn sleigh for hire."

Nina's heart skipped. The tree lighting was one
of Kringle's most romantic holiday traditions.
"Like... like a date?" she asked, hardly daring to
believe it.

Ryan held her gaze. "Yeah, exactly like a date.
If you want it to be, that is."

"I'd love to, Ryan. It sounds perfect." She
pressed a palm to her chest and smiled up at him.

"Great, I'll pick you up at six?"

Feeling giddy, Nina nodded. "Six it is."

"Since we're both headed in the same direction, would you mind if I followed you home, just
to make sure you get there safely?"

Touched by his concern, she nodded. "I'd like
that."

Why had he asked her on a date?

Ryan couldn't answer the question as he
followed Nina's truck down the quiet streets of
Kringle. The night air pressed heavy around him.

His pulse, still unsettled from the leftover adrenaline of catching her when she fell from that ladder, rippled.

That closeness, the way she'd looked up at him with such utter trust, shook him in unexpected ways.

Ahead, Nina's taillights blinked. She turned into her neighborhood and pulled into a driveway. Her house. He'd never known where she lived. It was a modest cottage but with quaint architecture that had a welcoming feel. Christmas lights decorated the eaves, and in the front window, a tree glowed. A simple but unmistakable picture of home, the kind of place where one might kick off their shoes and sink onto a plush sofa with a peaceful sigh.

His place? It was anything but.

Ten miles away, his ranch waited, dark and empty, with no signs of life except the cattle in the pasture. He hadn't even left the Christmas lights on. His house felt more like a relic of the past, every room filled with memories he didn't want to confront. After his parents passed and Jenny married and left, the house wasn't a home anymore, just a shell where he slept and worked.

And tonight, the difference fully hit him hard.

Nina's home was lively, rich, and inviting. The thought of her stepping inside, putting on some Christmas music and brewing herself a cup of bedtime herbal tea, stirred something in him. It wasn't jealousy—it was a hollow feeling, a reminder of what he'd been avoiding for years.

His hands tightened on the steering wheel. What was he doing, trailing after her like this? He'd told himself that keeping his distance was the smart move, that a woman like Nina had her whole future ahead of her, but the truth was, he was the one who'd kept himself stuck. Working the ranch, burying himself in routine, avoiding anything that made him feel too much.

And Nina? She was making him feel everything.

He parked at the end of her driveway, watching as she got out of her van. She paused for a moment, glancing back toward him before giving a little wave, and then she slipped inside her house.

The door clicked shut behind her, leaving Ryan in the quiet of the street, staring after her.

He leaned back in his seat, the engine still running, his eyes drifting to the rearview mirror.

His reflection stared back at him, tense and

conflicted. He'd spent so long keeping everything and everyone at arm's length, locking away his emotions because it was easier, but this wasn't easy anymore.

Nina brought something back to life in him—something he wasn't sure he could handle.

Could he really risk getting close to her? What if she decided this town—or worse, he—wasn't enough? The thought of her walking away cut more profound than he cared to admit. And yet the idea of going back to that empty, lifeless house, of continuing to pretend that the loneliness didn't get to him, felt unbearable.

The question gnawed at him as he stared down the road leading back to the ranch. For the first time in a long while, the notion of heading home alone left him unsettled.

Was this it? The moment when he finally stopped hiding, stopped letting the past control every decision? Or would he continue down this road of isolation and regret?

His eyes flicked once more to the rearview mirror, but this time, he wasn't just seeing himself. He was seeing the man he had the potential to be—the man who could take a risk, who could let someone in again, who could finally let go of the fear that had kept him paralyzed for far too long.

But that kind of change wouldn't be easy. It never was. And Nina... she might be the biggest risk of all.

CHAPTER 9

IN THE BAKERY kitchen the following morning, Nina kneaded a batch of sourdough, her last of the morning. Business had picked up the last couple of days, thank heavens.

A lock of hair fell loose from her bun and drooped into her eyes. Laughing, she blew it back from her face. Still giddy from the previous night, she sang "Christmas Cookies" under her breath.

She had a date. A *real*, official date with Ryan Danvers for tomorrow night. Her Christmas dream was coming true.

Today, Gee staffed the front counter, and his welcoming voice drifted into the kitchen. "How's the arthritis treating you, Ruth?"

"Thank you for asking, Dr. Ellis," Mrs. Claiborne said. "That Arthur Itis is a right constant pain, but I'm used to him. He lets me know I'm still alive. Give me a loaf of honey wheat and half a dozen black and white cookies, will you?"

"Sure thing."

"Nina!" Ruth called, leaning around the counter to wave at her through the kitchen entrance. "I want to thank you again for helping out at the church last night. That angel looks stunning, and she's a perfect addition to our pageant."

Nina stuck her head into the storefront, her hands caked with flour. "My pleasure. Glad I could help. I hope the pageant draws a standing-room-only crowd."

The jingle bells above the door jangled, and Nina glanced over to see who'd arrived.

Katherine Brothers stepped inside, as chicly dressed as before, and she got in line behind the last customer.

Nina's stomach dropped. Uh-oh, what was *that* woman doing here? She rushed to the kitchen sink to wash the flour from her hands and popped back into the storefront just as Katherine reached the counter.

"I've got this, Gee." Nina took hold of her grandfather's shoulders and propelled him toward the kitchen. "Will you take the brownies out of the oven for me, please?"

Gee shook his head and blinked. "I-I... why can't you just take them out?"

"Please," she said. "For me?"

He shot her a puzzled expression but nodded and trailed into the kitchen.

Breathless, Nina turned to Katherine. "How may I help you?"

Katherine flicked a gaze around the bustling bakery. All the tables and chairs were full, and the line behind the woman grew as more customers came in and set the bells jingling again.

"Separating me from your grandfather?" Katherine asked.

"What?" Nina feigned surprise. "No."

"Business has picked up." A pleased look came over Katherine's face. "That's nice to see."

"What did you need?" Nina asked, trying to cut the woman off at the pass. "Bread, cookies, pies?"

"Actually, I wanted to discuss the text you sent me."

"As you can see, we're swamped, so if you don't have an order to place..." Nina waved toward the door. She shot a look over her shoulder to see Gee standing in the doorway between the storefront and the kitchen, watching her interaction with Katherine.

Undaunted, Nina addressed the customer in line behind Katherine. "What'll you have, Mrs. Pierson?"

"I just need a minute of your time," Katherine said, persisting.

Gee came over. "What's going on, Nina?"

Briefly, Nina closed her eyes, collecting herself.

Katherine held out her hand to Gee. "Hello, Mr. Ellis. I'm Katherine Brothers. Nice to meet you."

Gee shook her hand. "Welcome to Ellis Early Eats, Ms. Brothers. What can we do for you?"

Katherine transferred her gaze back to Nina. "Your granddaughter didn't tell you about me?"

Now Gee was staring at Nina, too. "No," he said, stroking his jaw. "She didn't."

Nina let out a sigh and sagged against the counter. "I have customers."

"I need a dozen Parker rolls," Mrs. Pierson said. "And a fruitcake."

Nina moved to fill Mrs. Pierson's order, wishing Katherine Brothers would just go away.

Katherine moved aside to let Mrs. Pierson up

to the counter, but she didn't leave. Instead, she kept talking to Gee. "Mr. Ellis, I offered to purchase the bakery from your granddaughter a few days ago. She turned me down, but I was hoping to speak to you since you're the owner on record and plead my case."

Gee frowned. "Offer? What offer?"

Katherine mentioned the purchase amount she'd told Nina, and Gee's eyes widened.

He swung toward Nina. "Why didn't you tell me?"

"I'll leave you two to discuss," Katherine Brothers said, looking pleased with herself. "You have my number, Nina."

She walked out, leaving Nina with shaky legs and a sinking heart.

Gee took over the checkout, handling Mrs. Pierson's purchase as Nina boxed her baked goods.

"As soon as things slow down," he said. "You and I are gonna have a long chat, granddaughter."

───

The bakery was finally quiet. The last customer had left, and the chairs were flipped up on the tables, ready for the morning rush. Garrett sat at the kitchen table, sipping his coffee and glancing at the plate of cookies between him and Nina. His legs ached more than usual these days, and he couldn't help but notice how much more tired he felt after a long day.

He picked up a black and white cookie, bit into it, and savored the sweetness. "These turned out extra good today. Just the right amount of frosting. You do Ellie proud."

The mention of his late wife, Ellie, always made him pause. This bakery had been her dream. She was the one who loved every corner of it, from the smell of fresh dough to the smiles on the customers' faces. Garrett had stayed because it was her passion, not his. The family kept the bakery going after she passed because selling the bakery meant letting go of Ellie.

But now? A lot of time had passed, and things had changed. His son and daughter-in-law had moved off to Arizona, leaving Nina at the helm with a bit of help from Garrett. His granddaughter had readily shouldered the burden, but had they all put too much on her slender shoulders?

Nina smiled, but it didn't reach her eyes. She was distracted, her fingers tracing the rim of her coffee mug. Garrett knew that look—she was lost in thought, worrying about one thing or another. Even when she was a little girl, she took on more than her share of responsibility.

"Honey?" He reached across the table to touch her hand. "You okay?"

Her eyes met his, weighed with exhaustion. "Just tired. The holiday rush takes it out of me."

He set his cookie down and cut straight to it. "So," he said, "this offer from Katherine Brothers... Why did you hide it from me?"

Nina's shoulders stiffened. She cradled her mug closer, staring down at it. "I didn't want to trouble you with it. We're not selling, no matter how much she offers."

He rubbed between his eyes with the pad of his thumb. His granddaughter looked smaller as if she'd shrunk somehow. "You love the bakery that much?"

She nodded and raised her head to meet his gaze. "Gramma loved it."

"That's not what I asked."

"I love honoring Gramma's memory."

"That's not the same thing as loving being a baker."

"It's all I know," she said.

"You've never had time to explore anything else.

I think selling the bakery is something we should talk about. This place... it's a lot of work, Nina. And I'm not getting any younger. Soon, it will all be on you, and we just don't have the money for you to hire help. I hate to see you work yourself into the ground for something that's not *your* passion."

"But selling it feels like surrender, you know?"

"Like finally admitting Ellie is gone?" he asked.

She nodded, her fingers tightened around the mug, and she blinked rapidly. "Yeah."

"Letting go is hard," he murmured. "But your grandmother didn't expect you to keep her dream going. It was her dream. I'm not sure it's yours."

"It's not, not my dream," she said. "And the bakery is a centerpiece of the town square."

"Wouldn't it still be so with Katherine Brothers as the owner?"

"She did offer me a salary to stay on as manager and I could hire staff. I wouldn't have to get up at three in the morning. I could finally have a social life."

"Something you might consider since you and Ryan Danvers have been eyeballing each other."

"Gee!"

"What? I'm not blind, girl. The man is interested, and if I'm not mistaken, you're interested right back."

She surrendered a shy smile. "I am."

"Well, then..." He paused. "You'll be twenty-six in a few months. It's time to start thinking about what *you* really want out of life."

"What about you and Jean Deerling?" Nina asked.

"She invited me to go to Padre Island with her for Valentine's Day."

Nina lit up. "Are you going?"

"I didn't want to leave you alone at the bakery for four days, so I told her no."

"Gee, forget about me. You should go if that's what you want," Nina said. She met his gaze. "I like her."

Garrett pressed his mouth straight, suppressing the smile that wanted to spread over his face at the thought of Jean. "I do, too."

"So you want me to sell the bakery?"

"It is a lot of money."

"That doesn't answer my question."

"I love this bakery and the memories our family created here, but it's not mine like it was Ellie's. And I don't want you feeling like you have to carry it all on your shoulders, Nina. If selling makes things easier, I'll back you up."

For a moment, Nina didn't say anything. She just stared into her coffee, her face unreadable. Then, slowly, her lower lip trembled. She caught it between her teeth. "I'm not sure I'm ready to let it go, but Katherine's offer... it would take some of the pressure off. It's been hard, Gee. I didn't want to admit it, but it's been tough."

"It's okay to let it be hard," he said. "But it's also okay to move on. Sometimes, letting go doesn't mean giving up. It means making room for something else."

Nina let out a shaky breath. Her eyes clouded with uncertainty. "I'm torn."

"It's not a decision to make likely. Don't rush it." He sent her a bittersweet smile, feeling nostalgia curl up against his heart. "Whatever you choose, I'll back you up one hundred percent."

Nina pushed back her chair. "C'mon," she said. "I'll drive you home. There's rain on the way and with the temperature dropping, it could easily turn to sleet. I want to be in front of a cozy fire with hot cocoa and a Hallmark Christmas movie on when it rolls in."

Ryan woke thinking of Nina and their date that evening. He had a lot to do to get ready. First, his chores, then head to Kringle for a haircut. His hair was getting shaggy, and he wanted to look his best for her. He also had a few more party supplies to pick up before the Christmas party next weekend.

His thoughts traveled back to Nina and the church potluck. He recalled how the red and green holiday lights shone against her glossy black hair as they shared a meal at the communal table and how pretty her lips had looked, slick with pearly pink lipstick.

He dressed, drank a cup of coffee, and pulled out his phone, tempted to text her.

But what would he say? *Good morning, gorgeous* seemed too forward. The last thing he wanted was to scare her off. He set his phone on the counter and refilled his coffee mug.

It had drizzled last night, and the freezing temperatures formed icy patches over the porch and yard. Gingerly, he picked his way down the steps and across the yard to the barn, his mind jettisoning unbidden back to Nina.

Ryan breathed in the crisp air. He had been

looking forward to this date ever since he worked up the courage to ask Nina to the tree lighting ceremony.

Mentally, he ran through his to-do list. Feed the horses, check on the pregnant heifer in the south pasture, and repair the fence near the creek. Then into town for that haircut and pick up the last of the decorations for the party. He hoped he had time to stop by the bakery and maybe say hi to Nina before their date.

Lost in thought, Ryan wasn't paying attention and his bootheel hit a patch of hidden ice.

His coffee mug thrust upward into the air, flinging hot liquid over his coat. One leg flew out from under him. He struggled for balance, but his other leg twisted beneath him, and he heard a loud *pop* and landed flat on his back.

For a moment, he stared, stunned, at the sunrise. The cold from the frozen ground seeped through his clothes, chilling him to the bone.

Ryan lay there for several minutes, catching his breath and taking stock of the pain and his injury. His knee throbbed a sharp, insistent pain that made him grit his teeth. He tried to flex his foot, but a fresh wave of agony washed over him.

He struggled to push himself up, but his knee

hurt so bad he flopped back down, huffing out big gulps of air. Too bad he'd given the ranch hands two weeks off. No one would come across him. He'd have to call for help.

Grunting against the pain, he fumbled in the pocket of his shearling coat, looking for his phone, and that's when he realized he left it on the kitchen counter.

Son of a mangy biscuit eater.

The ground beneath him was colder than he would've thought possible. Melting sleet gave him the sort of injury he'd always expected to come from an opposing cornerback when he quarter-backed for the Kringle Yellow Jackets.

Yikes.

He glanced across the length of the yard between the barn and the house. It was a good hundred yards. With the throbbing in his knee, it would take hours to drag himself that far.

No one would come looking for him. Jenny was at home on bed rest. Scott was out of town for work. The ranch hands were all on vacation.

He was stuck. With a groan, he closed his eyes.

So much for his date with Nina.

CHAPTER 10

NINA WIPED down the bakery counter after the lunch rush, trying to decide what to wear on her date with Ryan. Maybe something red that contrasted with her dark hair and pale skin. Mom said red was "her" color, and it fit the season.

The tree-lighting ceremony was just a few hours away, and she couldn't wait to spend the evening with him. At long last. A date with Ryan Danvers.

A few diners lingered, finishing off their sandwiches. The bakery closed at two thirty, and it was now one forty-five.

The landline mounted on the wall next to the display case rang. Nina leaned over to snag the receiver from its cradle.

"Ellis Early Eats, Nina speaking. How may I help you?"

"Nina, this is Jenny Finley, Ryan's sister."

Why was Jenny calling her? Nina put a hand to her chest. Was Ryan backing out of their date? Had he put his sister up to breaking the news?

"Y-yes?" Gak! Why did she sound so shaky and unsure of herself?

"I really hate to bother you, but I was wondering if you've heard from Ryan today?"

"No." Not knowing what else to say, Nina pulled her bottom lip up between her teeth. "Is there a problem?"

Jenny sighed. "I'm not sure. I've been trying to reach him all morning, but he's not answering his phone. The ranch hands are off for Christmas and he's all alone out there on the ranch, and I just can't shake this uneasy feeling."

Was something amiss, or was Jenny's imagination in overdrive because of pregnancy hormones and bed rest? Nina's pulse pumped harder. She didn't want to be dismissive of the woman's concerns.

"I called his neighbor to go check on him but didn't realize the family was skiing in Aspen for the holidays. I'd send Scott over, but he's out of town on business for a couple of days." Anxiety tinged Jenny's voice. "I hate to ask, but since you and Ryan have plans later today—"

"Ryan told you about that?" Inordinately pleased that he'd discussed their date with his sister, Nina smiled.

"Oh yes. My brother came by to check on me last night, and he was singing your praises."

Nina curled her toes inside her ankle boots and pressed her palm to her mouth to keep from laughing out loud.

"Would you mind terribly going out to check on him? I know I'm probably jumping at shadows, but it's unlike Ryan not to answer his phone. I'd go myself, but the doctor's orders..."

"Of course," Nina said. "I'll head over there right away."

"Thank you, Nina. You're a lifesaver. Please let me know as soon as you know anything."

"Will do." Nina hung up the receiver and turned to find Gee watching her with a raised eyebrow.

"What's up?" he asked.

Nina explained the situation. "I need to go check on Ryan. Can you close up?"

"Sure, sure."

Gee nodded, a knowing smile playing at the corners of his mouth. "Go on, I've got this covered. You go make sure that boy's alright."

"Thanks." She kissed her grandfather's cheek, took off her apron, and grabbed her coat. She tried not to jump to conclusions, but she couldn't help worrying about Ryan.

The drive to the Danvers ranch seemed an eternity, even though it was only ten miles outside of town. Nina's mind raced with possibilities. Maybe Ryan had just fallen asleep with his phone on silent. Or perhaps he was out in one of the far pastures, out of cell range. Still, as the ranch came into view, worry tightened in her chest.

She pulled up to the sprawling farmhouse and killed the engine. Ryan's truck sat parked in the driveway. The sun was out now, the earlier ice having melted away, leaving everything slightly damp and earthy-smelling.

Nina got out and walked up the front porch, the wooden steps creaking beneath her feet. She knocked on the door, the sound echoing in the stillness.

No answer.

She rang the doorbell.

Still nothing.

"Ryan?" She moved to press her face to the window and peered inside the living room. No one around.

Nina stepped back, bit her lip, and glanced around the property. The ranch lay quiet—too quiet. Where could he be?

Maybe the barn? Perhaps that was it. He was prepping for the party. Made total sense. But why hadn't he answered his phone?

Following her instincts, she headed for the barn. The double doors pushed apart slightly.

"Ryan?" she called again, feeling as if she were trespassing. "Are you out there?"

"Nina!" Relief flooded Ryan's voice. "In here!"

She shoved the heavy rolling double doors all the way open and rushed inside. Her chest squeezed tight.

The scent of hay filled her nostrils, along with a sharp note of sweat that cut through the usual barn smells.

She heard a low groan.

She moved around the door and spied Ryan propped against the wall, his broad shoulders hunched, face pale, perspiration beading his brow, his body curled protectively around his right leg.

"Ryan!" She sprang to his side.

He glanced up at her, trying to smile through a grimace, his dark-brown eyes tinged with pain.

Nina knelt next to him and hovered a hand at his shoulder. "What happened?"

His jaw muscle twitched. "I slipped on the ice this morning and bunged up my knee. It was closer to drag myself into the barn than the house."

"Oh my gosh, you've been here for hours!"

"Made myself useful, though." He winced and waved a hand at the stacked cardboard boxes. "I untangled all the Christmas lights."

Indeed, a myriad of string lights lay neatly wound into circles around him.

"Oh my stars!" She glanced down at his leg, noticing the swollen knee beneath his jeans. Loose hay clung to his coat and hair, and she resisted the urge to brush it away. Instead, she assessed the situation, her mind racing with worry and the need to help.

"I'm sorry," he said. "I'm not sure I can keep our date."

"Ya think?"

He gave her such a mournful look it hurt her heart.

"How long have you been here? Why didn't you call for help?"

Ryan sighed, wincing as he tried to shift his position. "Like a doofus, I left my phone in the house."

"Can you stand?"

"I haven't tried lately. My confounded knee swelled so fast I couldn't bend it through my jeans, and every time I tried to get up, I kept falling on my backside. Finally, I just gave up."

She clucked her tongue. "You must be freezing."

"Thirsty, too."

She shrugged off her coat and draped it over him. "We need to get you to a doctor. Let's try to get you up."

Ryan attempted to sit up but fell back with a hiss of pain.

"Scale of one to ten, how bad does it hurt?"

"When I'm just sitting here, five-ish. But when I try to move, we're looking at eight to nine."

Nina chewed her lower lip, thinking fast. "Okay, don't try to move. I'll call Gee. He'll know what to do."

She pulled out her phone and dialed her grandfather's number, explaining the situation as soon as he picked up.

"Keep him still and try to elevate his leg if you can," Gee said. "I'll close up the bakery and be there as soon as I can. In the meantime, keep him warm and comfortable."

Nina ended the call and turned back to Ryan. "Gee's on his way. He says we should elevate your leg. Do you think you can scoot back a bit? There's a hay bale we could use to prop up your foot."

Ryan nodded, gritting his teeth, and they maneuvered him into a better position. Nina gathered some loose hay to cushion his injured knee, then carefully lifted his leg onto the hay bale.

"How's that?"

"Better," Ryan said, though his voice came out strained. "Thank you."

She settled down beside him, taking his hand in hers. "Jenny was worried when she couldn't reach you. I need to call her, by the way."

Ryan squeezed her hand, a look of guilt crossing his face. "I didn't mean to worry anyone. I just... I felt so stupid lying out here. I thought I could handle it on my own."

"You don't have to handle everything on your

own, Ryan. That's what friends are for. That's what I'm here for."

"Friends?" he said lightly. "Is that what we are?"

"I hope so." She met his gaze.

"I was hoping for more."

Her pulse skittered. "Me too," she whispered.

He squeezed her hand.

She squeezed his right back.

Before long, a vehicle pulled into the driveway.

"That'll be Gee," she said and hopped up. She went to the barn door and waved to her grandfather as he got out of his truck, medical bag in hand.

Gee came into the barn, examined Ryan's leg, and shook his head. "This is beyond what I can do here. I'm afraid it's time to call an ambulance. You're gonna need surgery, son."

Ryan winced but nodded, clearly trying to brace himself for what was coming. Nina felt a surge of sympathy rise inside her. She stayed close, squeezing his hand once more as Gee made the call.

"I'll be fine, Nina," Ryan said.

She smiled, though her heart still thudded fast. "You're not getting out of our date that easily."

Ryan chuckled despite the pain. "I'll hold you to that."

The ambulance ride felt like a blur, a haze of concerned faces and flashing lights. Ryan's knee throbbed with every bump in the road, each jolt sending a fresh wave of pain through his body.

Through it all, Nina stayed by his side, her hand in his, anchoring him. Her touch was warm against his clammy skin, her fingers intertwined with his, offering silent support.

Even as the paramedics wheeled him into the Fort Worth hospital, she remained a constant presence. The harsh fluorescent lights cast shadows under her eyes, highlighting the worry etched across her face. Yet her voice remained steady, a soothing balm amidst the hubbub of the emergency room.

Nina called Jenny and kept his sister updated, but Ryan barely registered it.

The surgery passed in a fog of anesthesia and discomfort. As consciousness slipped away, the last thing Ryan remembered was Nina's voice, promising she'd be there when he woke up.

It was a promise she kept, her face the first thing he saw as he blinked back to awareness in the sterile hospital room. Her smile, tired but relieved, was like sunlight breaking through clouds.

Now, back at the ranch, the familiar smells of home greeted him—wood polish, fresh air, and the distant scent of hay. But there was something else, too, a hint of vanilla and cinnamon that he'd come to associate with Nina. It mingled with the antiseptic smell that clung to his skin, a reminder of the hospital they'd left behind.

The doctors released him early Sunday morning, deeming him "cleared" to go, though the word felt generous. His knee, wrapped tight in bandages, throbbed with every heartbeat, a constant reminder of his vulnerability. The pain medication dulled the edge but couldn't erase it completely.

The ride back to the ranch turned out much quieter than the frantic journey to the hospital. Nina drove while he stretched out in the back seat of her car. Her eyes flicked between watching him in her rearview mirror and the road as she navigated the country lanes.

Ryan's thoughts had wandered during the drive, fixating on his knee, on his frustration, and on the doctor's insistence that he couldn't be left alone for the next few days. The idea of dependence grated against his every instinct. He was used to being the one others relied on, not the other way around.

Now, he lay in his parents' old bedroom, feeling the weight of the past settle over him. He looked around the familiar space, taking in details. The old oak dresser still stood against the far wall, its surface now bare of the trinkets and photos that once cluttered it. The curtains were the same faded floral print his mother had loved, now drawn back to let in the late morning sunlight.

Ryan wanted to be upstairs in his own room, surrounded by his things, but he knew it would be days before he could manage the stairs. So here he was, stuck in this room that held so many echoes of the past.

Nina offered alternatives—the couch in the den, the one in the living room, even suggesting he stay with her, but in the end, practicality won out.

This room was spacious, the bed more comfortable than anything in the den, and Jenny insisted he use it, her text message brooking no argument.

That had settled it. Ryan didn't want to upset his sister, but now, lying in his parents' bed, dressed in his sheets, comforter, and pillows—all thanks to Nina's thoughtfulness—he felt a strange blend of comfort and unease.

The familiar creaks of the old house surrounded him, each sound triggering a memory. The distant tick of the grandfather clock in the hallway, the whisper of wind through the oak trees outside—it was all achingly familiar, yet somehow foreign after so long.

Nina hovered nearby, tucking sheets and adjusting pillows with care that both touched and irritated him.

Her movements were gentle, almost reverent as if she understood the emotional weight of this room. She was doing too much, fussing like he was helpless, and it made him grumpy.

Not because he didn't appreciate the help—he did, more than he could express—but because he was used to doing things on his own.

Being incapacitated and feeling dependent, it all went against the grain of who he was. Years of running the ranch ingrained in him a fierce independence that was hard to let go of, even when he knew he needed the help. And worse, he hated being at her mercy. Even though, deep down, a part of him recognized that if he could just relax and let go of his stubborn pride for a moment, it might not be so bad.

But relaxation had never been his strong suit, especially not here, in this room filled with memories. Every glance around the space brought a new recollection—his mother's laugh, his father's firm but gentle hand on his shoulder, family gatherings and quiet moments alike.

"The way I see it, you're lucky to have me," Nina said, her voice pulling him from his thoughts as she shoved an extra pillow behind his back. Her tone was light, teasing, but there was an undercurrent of genuine concern that Ryan couldn't miss. "Doctor said you need to rest as much as possible, remember?"

He eyed her, a mix of gratitude and frustration warring within him. The sunlight streaming through the window caught in her black hair, highlighting strands of deep navy he'd never noticed before.

"I have crutches, and I'm not helpless," he grumbled, then added softly, "And thanks." The words felt inadequate, but they were all he could manage.

"Crutches or not, you need to rest," Nina replied, her hands on her hips as she arched a brow at him, mimicking the doctor's stern authority. The playful glint in her eye betrayed her amusement at the situation, softening the reprimand. "Doctor's orders."

Ryan leaned back with a huff, more out of defeat than anything else. Not that he'd admit it. "You sure those aren't sister's orders?"

Nina's lips twitched into a smile, refusing to rise to the bait. Instead, she turned and picked up a plate from the bedside table, balancing a fork on the edge. "Blueberry cinnamon rolls, fresh from the bakery. Now, don't say I never did anything for you."

The scent hit him before he even took the plate, rich and sweet, a reminder of simpler times. She had gone to the bakery while he was being poked, prodded, and x-rayed, made sure he'd have meals lined up for the day—all without him asking. The smell of cinnamon and berries rose from the plate, but what really struck him was how much she had done. All before noon.

Ryan let out a long breath, feeling the tension in his chest unravel just a little. He looked up at her, really looked at her, taking in the soft curves of her face, the wisps of hair that had escaped her hasty ponytail. He wanted to get this next part right because it mattered. Because she mattered.

"Nina," he said, his voice quieter now, serious. "I wouldn't say that. You've become more a part of my life than anyone else, except my parents and Jenny and Scott." The words felt heavy with meaning, with everything left unsaid between them.

Her smile softened, her wide mouth quirking at the edges, that too-knowing look in her eyes. "Good. Don't forget it."

There was a tenderness in her voice that made his heart skip.

Ryan couldn't help smiling back, even through the discomfort. He would never in a million years forget Nina Ellis, not a single detail. Not the way she hummed under her breath when she thought no one was listening, or how her eyes crinkled at the corners when she laughed, or the fierce determination she showed in everything she did.

He stared at her for a moment longer, something pulling at him from deep within, something unplanned and overwhelming.

"Can you stay?" The words came out before he could stop them, surprising even himself with their vulnerability.

Nina stilled, her hands hovering midair over

the blankets she had been straightening. For a beat, she didn't speak, and Ryan felt his heart hammering in his chest.

Had he overstepped? Asked too much? But then, with a soft look in her eyes that made his breath catch, she nodded.

"Of course," she said, her voice barely above a whisper. "I'll stay as long as you need."

CHAPTER 11

STAY.

Ryan wanted her to stay. He'd asked her to stay.

More than anything, Nina wanted to do just that, but she needed to know what he meant.

What he really wanted from her. What he expected. If anything, at all. And if she'd be comfortable with whatever "it" turned out to be.

Standing at the side of the bed, Nina studied the fine lines at the corners of his eyes and those bracketing his mouth.

He was in more pain than he let on. Big bad cowboy. She suppressed a smile. Levity was out of place right now.

The clock on the wall ticked loudly in the quiet

room. Nina traced the patchwork pattern on the faded quilt, her gaze fixed on Ryan's face. The sun filtering in through the blinds cast shadows across the bed, highlighting his handsome features.

Her breath grew shallow. She was here with Ryan Danvers. Alone. In a bedroom.

"Forgive me." He squeezed his eyes shut and shook his head before opening them again. "That wasn't clear. *I* wasn't clear. I don't mind being alone. I'm a capable adult."

"I know."

He gave a half-hearted chuckle. "Most of the time, anyway. It would be nice to have someone in the house in case... well, I fall again getting up to go to the bathroom."

Nina dropped her hand from the quilt and stepped back from the bed. "Reasonable request. Why had she thought his reason for asking would be anything else? "I truly don't mind staying. The bakery is closed on Sundays."

"Is today Sunday?" He seemed confused.

"Yes."

"But it's your only day off."

She shrugged. "This is more important." *You're more important.*

"But what about tomorrow? You get up at three a.m."

"You know what? It's my bakery. I can close up tomorrow, too."

"And disappoint your customers this close to Christmas? No, ma'am."

"You let me decide that, okay?"

Ryan frowned. "I don't want you to lose business because of me. I can't ask that."

"You didn't. I offered."

He looked weary and shoved a hand through his hair. "No. I'll be okay. I wasn't thinking. You've got work, your own responsibilities."

"It's fine. Seriously. I can stay until Scott returns from his business trip. Jenny says he'll be home tomorrow afternoon. I'm happy to stay." She was more than happy. The thought rocked her. She *wanted* to stay. Very much.

Why? That was the question. She didn't know what was happening here. They'd shared an impromptu dance, an angel mishap, and a potluck. Plus, she'd helped him when he got hurt. A week together. A matter of hours, all told. However, they had known each other for years. On the periphery, yes, but still.

But they hadn't been close until lately, and now she was tucking him in, spending the night—

Stop it, Nina.

"Listen, I'm glad to do it. I know you're a proud guy, and you don't like to ask for help, but we all need people from time to time. Besides, you'll owe me." She smiled to let him know she was teasing.

He shifted his knee on the pillow and let out a small groan.

She leaped to his side. "What can I do? What do you need?"

"I'm okay. Just a twinge."

"That did not sound okay." She flickered her gaze to the wall clock. "It's too soon for more pain meds, so maybe get some sleep?"

"I slept for twelve hours after surgery."

"Be that as it may, you need rest."

"What I need is a distraction," he mumbled.

What did he mean by that? She studied him.

His jaw clenched and unclenched, and his fingers plucked at the blanket. He *was* in pain, and she felt helpless. Not a favorite feeling of hers.

"You wanna watch a movie?" He waved at the large screen TV mounted on the wall.

"Um... okay." When had she last watched a

movie in the middle of the day? Years. "Do you want something to eat first?"

He nodded toward the plate with his cinnamon roll. "Delicious, by the way."

"I meant a proper lunch. Something substantial. I can see what's in your kitchen. If you've got eggs, I could make an omelet. Or popcorn if you have any... for the movie."

He laughed. "Food does sound pretty amazing."

"I'll put the news on and go see what I can find." She picked up the remote and switched on the TV. The familiar jingle of the local news station filled the room.

"Sounds good, but honestly, a PB&J and J sammie is fine. I've got the ingredients. I'm pretty easy to please. I feel bad asking you to work. I really just wanted your company."

"Let me see what I can do," she said, her pulse fluttering as his words bounced around, echoing softly in her head before settling deep inside her heart.

Ryan scrolled through the endless queue of movies on the screen, his thumb flicking up and down on the remote. Titles blurred together, none of them registering. He wasn't in the mood for any of them.

All he could think about was Nina—just a few steps away in the kitchen. The sounds of her moving around—opening cabinets, rummaging in drawers, and the soft thud of the refrigerator door closing—floated into the bedroom.

Unaccustomed sounds. The house was usually quiet, silent, but now, it was alive, and it was all because of her.

Nina.

He pictured her moving gracefully through his space, her bare feet padding against his floor. Her hair pulled back, that rich dark shade catching the light. He liked having her here. In his house. His space.

It didn't feel invasive like he thought it might. If anything, it felt... right.

He hadn't planned on asking her to stay, but the words had come out before he could think them through. She could've said no, could've left him to his stubborn self-reliance. But she hadn't. And now, here she was, rearranging her life to take care of him.

He set the remote down, leaned back against the pillows, and rubbed his hand over his jaw. His knee throbbed beneath the blanket, but that wasn't the discomfort weighing on him. It was something else.

Something... deeper.

What was he doing? He wasn't the type to rely on anyone. He'd survived worse on his own, hadn't he? He could've managed—maybe with a little more effort, but he'd get by. And yet all he felt was relief she was here.

He let out a long breath, his thoughts tangling in unfamiliar knots. He wanted her to stay. Not because he needed someone to help him get through the next few days but because it was her.

Nina.

The woman who filled his house with warmth and made it feel like something other than just four walls.

The truth, the one he'd been avoiding all day, stared him in the face.

He wanted to be with her.

Simple raw fact. Yet the realization churned in his chest. Something far more complicated surged. He wasn't used to feeling this pull, this need to have her close. It unsettled him. Made him feel exposed.

Because if he admitted that he wanted her long-term, what would happen next? What did that mean for them?

Nina was smart, independent, and perfectly capable of moving on with her own life if she wanted. He wouldn't blame her if she did. Ryan wasn't exactly good at letting people in. In fact, he was terrible at it. His track record spoke for itself. The last thing he wanted was to pull her into something messy, something unfinished.

Yet despite all that logic telling him to back off, to keep his distance, here he was. Asking her to stay. Letting her care for him. Maybe even needing her.

He ran his hand over the arm of the quilt his grandmother had made, the soft fabric grounding him for a moment. Nina's presence in his house wasn't just about helping him. It was about *her*. About how she made him feel—steady, understood, seen.

And it wasn't just physical attraction, though that was part of it for sure. He wanted her, yes, but it went deeper than that. Whenever she was around, that gnawing ache he'd been carrying for years—the one that had settled in after his parents' death, after Jenny married and moved out, after the world seemed to move on without him—quieted.

She was staying the night. In his house. Under his roof. Something about that filled a hole he hadn't known existed. He wasn't alone. For the first time in a long time, he wasn't alone in this house, in his life.

But that scared him.

Because if he wasn't careful, he could get used to this—having her here, taking comfort in her presence. And what if that didn't last? What if she saw the cracks, the parts of him he kept hidden, and decided he wasn't worth it?

He could hear her humming faintly now, the gentle sound reaching him from the kitchen. He closed his eyes, letting her voice wash over him. For tonight, for now, she was here. He could let himself have this just for a little while. He could let her in, even if it was temporary.

Ryan opened his eyes. The sound of Nina's voice lifted in song to a Christmas ditty floated through the doorway, light and soft, and something inside him loosened. He'd been holding on way too tightly to the past for way too long.

Nina slipped into the bedroom, carrying a tray of food.

Ryan sat propped up against the pillows, his eyes on the TV, where *It's a Wonderful Life* played in black and white. But he seemed to stare straight through the screen instead of watching the ubiquitous holiday movie.

She set the tray on the bedside table. "Nothing fancy, just pasta, olive oil, lemon juice and cheese, but it should taste better than hospital food."

Ryan glanced at her, then back at the screen. "Thanks."

Nina took a seat on the edge of the bed, careful not to disturb him too much. She wasn't sure how to bridge the distance between them.

"Are you having some, too?" he asked.

"I am." She smiled at him and picked up a bowl. "I'm starving."

She got him situated and sat in the chair beside the bed. They both turned toward the TV, where George Bailey was running through Bedford Falls, shouting his joy.

"I watch this every year," she said. "Always

makes me feel like... I don't know. Like everything will turn out okay."

Ryan didn't reply right away. He just twirled his fork in the pasta. "Yeah, something like that."

They fell into silence again, George's plaintive voice the only sound in the room. Nina took a breath, unsure if she should say more. The quiet between them wasn't exactly uncomfortable. There was something beneath it, something in the way Ryan kept looking away, his body tense.

Despite him asking her to stay, did he actually not want her here?

She took a bite of pasta. It turned out really good, but she couldn't enjoy it. The tension seemed to tighten, the distance between them widening.

On the TV, George Bailey stood on the bridge, staring down at the water.

"Is there..." She trailed off, wondering if she should let it go, but the heaviness in the room felt stifling. "Are you hurting? It's time for a pain pill if you want one."

"I'm trying to tough it out," he said.

"There's no honor in suffering."

"I don't know. Maybe I deserve the pain."

"Ryan!" she said, shocked. "You don't mean that."

"Forgive me," he said. "It's the damn movie."

She reached for the remote and muted the TV. "What's going on?"

He shook his head. "My parents... never mind."

"Okay, I won't push you to talk." She went back to her pasta but kept an eye on him from her peripheral vision. Something was definitely up.

They ate in silence for a few minutes, and then Ryan said, "This movie was playing when..." His voice caught.

"Shh, shh," she said. "You don't owe me any explanation."

"I was hanging the stockings when the sheriff deputies knocked on the door that Christmas Eve and *It's A Wonderful Life* was on. We watched it every year together." His voice sounded far away and tinny, as if he were speaking through a long metal tube.

A lump of sympathy clogged her throat. She didn't speak. Everyone in Kringle knew about his family tragedy, but no one really talked about it. She'd been away at college when the accident happened and never really learned the details.

"Jenny wasn't home. She was with Scott. I was alone. Just me."

"Oh, Ryan." Nina put a hand to her chest. "I'm so sorry."

"The thing is, it was supposed to have been me," he said.

"You?"

"*I* was supposed to go to town for the horse feed, but I had a cold, and Mom insisted I stay home." He hiccuped. "All my fault in the first place. I neglected to order the supplies when Dad told me to. I was too busy mooning over Mandy Cartwright, who broken up with me to date my best friend. Because of me, my folks got on the road that Christmas Eve... because of me, they never came home."

Nina sucked in her breath through clenched teeth. Was that why he isolated himself on the ranch? Why he didn't date much, as far as she knew? Was he punishing himself for an accident?

He was sitting straight up in bed, staring at the muted TV, his eyes drilling a hole in George Bailey.

The room seemed to close in on itself. Grow smaller. Shrink.

Grief *haunted* this man. His parents had been gone for seven years, and yet he was still stuck in the past, still reliving that horrendous Christmas.

Her heart broke for him.

Ryan's shoulders trembled. He turned his face away from her, but she could see the tightness in his jaw, the rigidity in his body.

Nina's instinct was to reach out, to do something, but she wasn't sure how. This was bone-deep anguish, and she didn't feel equipped to soothe him. What could she say?

Uncertain, she shifted closer, watching him, waiting for him to say more if he wanted to.

"If I hadn't been so girl crazy—" His voice cracked, and he stopped.

She didn't know why she did what she did next. She didn't think. She just reacted, her singular goal to ease his suffering.

Sliding into the bed beside him, careful of his leg, Nina reached out and wrapped her arms around him.

At first, he didn't respond—his body stiff, like he was barely holding himself together. But as she cradled him in her arms and murmured *shh, shh*, his tension ebbed away. His breathing slowed, and suddenly, the sobs came, deep and raw, breaking through the surface.

Nina pulled him closer, guided his head to her shoulder, and just squeezed him tight. She didn't think about what this meant or whether it was the right thing to do. She knew he needed someone to hold him, to let him fall apart without judgment.

His body trembled against hers, and she could feel the weight of everything he'd been carrying for years—the guilt, the grief, all of it pouring out.

"You couldn't have known," she whispered, her voice steady, though her heart ached for him. "It wasn't your fault, Ryan. You were young. You did your best."

He didn't answer, but his grip on her tightened, his fingers clutching her as if she were his only anchor.

She held him through it, her hands running gently over his back, her cheek resting against his hair. She didn't say anything else. She didn't need to. Words wouldn't fix what had happened, and she knew that. She was just here, in this moment, with him.

Slowly, his sobs quieted, though his breathing stayed uneven. His body, which had been so rigid with tension, began to relax, and the shaking eased. He didn't let go, though, didn't pull away. Nina kept her arms around him, unsure of what to do next but knowing this wasn't the time to leave him alone.

CHAPTER 12

NINA JOLTED AWAKE.

She grabbed for her phone. It wasn't on her bedside table. The table wasn't there either. And the bed she was in wasn't hers. Neither was the room, the house... She spent the night with Ryan Danvers.

Platonically.

If that was a thing with him.

She lay on her back, staring at the ceiling fan, waiting for her pounding heart to slow, which she doubted was going to happen, considering where she was and who she was with. The fan turned in a slow reverse pattern, pulling down warm air blown up from the central heat vents. The soft whir of the blades filled the silence, a constant rhythm that did little to calm her racing thoughts.

The unfamiliar shadows of the room loomed around her, shapes she couldn't quite make out in the pre-dawn darkness. A faint scent of leather and hay lingered in the air, mixed with something distinctly Ryan. She breathed it in, letting it settle in her lungs.

"Did I wake you?" Ryan's voice was deep, the words softly spoken, though not quite a whisper. The sound of it in the darkness sent a shiver down her spine.

Nina whispered back, her voice barely audible even to her ears. "No. I'm used to waking up to go to work. I don't even know what time it is."

Her phone charged on his bedside table using his charge cord. He rolled to the side to fetch it and hand it to her. Her fingers brushed his in the dark, the brief contact sending a jolt through her that had nothing to do with static electricity.

"Huh. I actually overslept." It was three thirty. "I'm usually at the bakery by now." She darkened the screen and slid the phone under her pillow, the cool metal a stark contrast to the warmth of the bed. "How's your knee?"

"It's okay." Ryan tucked an arm beneath his

head. The rustle of fabric against fabric seemed impossibly loud in the quiet room. "Hard to get comfortable. I'm a side sleeper, but it hurt less when I stayed on my back."

"Me, too. The side sleeping thing. But I'm comfortable." He waited as if letting that sink in, then said, "You can go back to sleep."

"I'm afraid my entire schedule would get thrown off if I did." Nina stifled a yawn, realizing just how true those words were. Her body was used to early mornings and long days, a routine as familiar as breathing.

"Yeah. Same here. I feel like I need to get to work. It's hard for me to do nothing."

She rolled to face him, stacking her hands under her cheek and keeping plenty of distance between them, which wasn't hard to do in the king-size bed. She'd enjoyed the extra body heat and listening to him breathe, feeling his weight on the mattress, knowing she wasn't alone. It was a comfort she hadn't realized she'd been missing.

"I know what you mean. I can't remember the last time I had nothing to do. Or even permitted myself to put what needed doing on hold just to breathe."

Ryan turned his head toward her and chuckled. "You have to schedule time to breathe?"

"Not literally, though it feels like it at times. I've worked in the bakery all my life except when I was at college. It's all I know." The words came out more wistful than she'd intended, a hint of something she usually kept buried.

"Do you regret it? Taking over the bakery?"

"That's a hard question to answer," she said, not sure if she knew what was the truth and what was the brave front she put on. The question hung in the air, heavier than it should have been. "If I'd known then what I know now, I might've made a different choice, but I'm not sure if that's the same as regret."

"There's a lot of pressure involved in taking on a legacy operation," he said. "I get that for sure. Just like you, I took over the family business."

She wasn't sure if he was expecting her to answer, but she nodded. She hadn't ever really made a conscious decision to be a baker. It seemed coded into her genetics, a path laid out for her before she could even walk.

Her mother married into the Ellis Early Eats family and resented that it took up so much time.

In the end, she'd been the one to decide to leave Kringle, even though it was Dad's health that spurred the move. The memory of that decision, of the arguments and tears that preceded it, still stung.

"What career path would you have taken if your parents hadn't..." She trailed off. Why was she bringing up that pain again? The words hung unfinished between them, heavy with implication.

For a long time, he said nothing. The silence stretched, filled only by the sound of their breathing and the steady whir of the ceiling fan.

"I wanted to play pro football. A long shot, I know, but that was my dream."

"What?" She propped up on her elbow and looked over at him. She couldn't see his face in the darkness. Just felt the shape of him. The revelation caught her off guard, adding a new dimension to the man.

"I got scouted my junior year of college. I'd planned to surprise my folks with the news at Christmas."

A rush of empathy filled her chest, along with amazement and a strange, excited pride that he'd come so close to playing football professionally. "Why didn't you take the opportunity after your parents..."

"I had to keep the ranch going. I dropped out of school."

This new information changed her view of him. It turned the whole of her knowledge into something more decadent, fuller and unexpected. He was so much more than she knew. The weight of his sacrifice settled over her, a tangible thing in the darkness between them.

"I don't know what to say."

"There's not really anything to say. Life is life." He went silent after that.

"Do you ever think what life would've been like if you hadn't stayed in Kringle?"

"No reason to, really," he said. "Clinging to pipe dreams only causes pain. Acceptance is a gift."

"Have you ever traveled?" she asked.

"No. Never been out of Texas."

"The only other state I've been in is Arizona to visit my folks," Nina said. "Sometimes I wonder what it would be like to see the world. To experience different cultures, taste exotic foods, see landmarks I've only read about in books."

He turned his head, then rolled on his side to face her and grunted as he adjusted his leg. "You sound like you've given this some thought."

"I have. Don't get me wrong, I love Kringle, but there's so much out there. Sometimes I feel like I'm missing out on something bigger."

Ryan chuckled softly. "I never really thought about it that way."

"Where would you go? If you could choose anywhere?" she asked, curiosity coloring her tone.

"A place I could travel on horseback," he said after a moment's consideration.

She reached over and touched his shoulder. "It's been ages since I've ridden."

"We could—" He stopped mid-sentence, then finished with a terse, "Never mind."

She cupped his cheek. "I'd love to go riding with you. Let's plan to do that once you're back in the saddle."

The stubble on his face was a careless sort of scruff, his jaw sharp, chin strong, and neck corded. The ridge of his collarbone defined beneath the fabric of his shirt. She wanted to run her fingertip along it.

He raised up on one elbow and leaned closer. It wasn't a threatening move or even insistent. It was hesitant, as if he was testing the resistance between them.

"I'd like to kiss you."

"I'd like for you to kiss me."

He moved nearer, bracing his weight on his elbows and forearms. He was so close and yet he wasn't touching her at all. His breath brushed her face, the heat of it warming her.

Even so, she shivered.

"Cold?"

She shook her head and lifted one hand to brush the hair falling over his forehead to the side.

"Nervous?"

She wasn't that, either. She wanted the touch of his mouth on hers. It was a gorgeous anticipation, the wait.

"Change your mind?"

"I haven't yet. But I might. If you don't get on with it."

He laughed, brushing the backs of his fingers over her upper arm, her shoulder. "I'm not much for rushing things."

A groan rolled from her belly to her throat, but she caught it before it escaped. The idea of him taking his time left her breathless, weak, and trembling. Gooseflesh pebbled her skin.

His eyes were focused so intently on hers that she wasn't sure she could move. She wasn't sure she wanted to move. She wasn't sure of anything right now.

Not even what she was doing. Or if this was what she wanted.

Even after telling herself it was the very thing.

—

"Ryan?"

"Yeah?"

"I need some answers."

Ryan felt a shift in Nina at the same time he saw it on her face in the glow from the nightlight. Her body beside his stiffened. Her expression darkened, her uneasiness evident, and filled with questions he wasn't sure he could answer even if she put them into words.

But he'd dang sure try. "What do you want to know?"

"Why I'm here. Not the part where I agreed to stay because you were hurt," she said, her tone lighter than the look in her eyes. "But why here? Beside you in this bed?" She paused, swallowed, and then whispered, "Why me, Ryan?"

Fair questions, mainly since neither one of

them dated much or lived the sort of life that had room for relationships.

Ryan's heart raced, the steady thrum echoing in his ears. The soft cotton sheets beneath them suddenly felt rough against his skin, his nerves hypersensitive to every sensation. The urge to feel her mouth on his had come out of nowhere.

No. That wasn't true.

He'd thought about kissing her a bunch of times. Dancing with her in the bakery, catching her when she fell from the ladder at the fellowship hall, frankly, anytime he peered into her milk chocolate brown eyes.

But the conversations they'd shared on those occasions, and the ones they'd had since, gave his desire a depth he wouldn't be able to keep out of a kiss.

A memory flashed through his mind—Nina laughing as she dusted flour from her hands, her eyes crinkling at the corners. Something shifted then, a realization that she was more than just the woman who made the best cinnamon rolls in Kringle. She was vibrant, full of life, and irresistible.

And he knew in his gut that would change everything.

It still wasn't easy to face.

"I've thought about kissing you since you asked me to dance to George Strait."

Nina's breath caught, the sound soft in the quiet room. "I've wondered about that. If it was just me who felt something powerful that day."

And here he'd thought he'd been wearing a neon sign. "Well, now you know. So because of that, I almost ran out of the church when I saw you were there to help with the pageant setup."

She reached for the sheet and pulled it up to her chin, the rustle of fabric loud in the stillness. "Why would you do that?"

He took a deep breath and exhaled, the scent of vanilla and cinnamon that always clung to Nina filling his senses. "I didn't want to mess things up."

"Mess what up?"

"Dumb, huh? Hard to mess up what's not there."

After a moment of uncomfortable silence, she rolled up to sit cross-legged, holding his pillow in her lap as if needing a barrier between them. The moonlight filtering through the blinds cast shadows across her face, highlighting the uncertainty in her eyes.

"Is that what you think? That there's nothing between us? That we're both imagining this?"

She was brave to ask the question. Ryan felt a surge of admiration for her courage, even as fear gnawed at his insides. Opening up, letting someone in. It went against every instinct he'd developed since losing his parents. But Nina... she made him want to try.

He didn't think he could say it. "Then? Maybe not. But now?" He shook his head, holding her gaze. Moonlight found its way into the room around the edges of the blinds and lit up her hair. "We're not imagining it. I just..."

"Just what?"

"I don't know what to do about it." The admission felt like ripping off a bandage, exposing a wound he'd long tried to ignore.

She let out a laugh, which wasn't what he'd expected at all. The sound cut through the tension, warm and genuine. "Spoken like a man who's never been in a long-term relationship before."

"I haven't been." It was an easy admission. "The ranch, the responsibilities... they've always come first."

"Neither have I." Nina's voice softened, a hint

of vulnerability creeping in. "The bakery's been my whole world for so long."

He let that settle, feeling a grin tug at his mouth. "We're a pair, huh?"

"I really hate feeling this old when I'm so young. My whole life is supposed to be ahead of me. And by life, I don't mean making blueberry cinnamon rolls."

"You make delicious ones," he said, which had her rolling her eyes before she fell to the side, laughing. He loved her laugh. He loved her openness, her honesty. He wondered if love at first sight was really a thing because he was starting to think it might be.

The thought both thrilled and terrified him. What would the folks in Kringle say if the reclusive rancher and the dedicated baker suddenly became an item? Would it change how they fit into the community? And, more importantly, was he ready to open himself up to the possibility of loss again?

"You know," Nina said, interrupting his thoughts, "for two people who run businesses, we're pretty terrible at taking risks in our personal lives."

Ryan chuckled, the tension easing a bit.

"Maybe we should treat this like a business decision. Weigh the pros and cons?"

Nina quirked an eyebrow. "Okay, I'll bite. Pro: we clearly enjoy each other's company."

"Con: we're both workaholics with no idea how to balance a relationship and our careers."

"Pro: we already know each other's quirks and still like each other."

"Con: the entire town will be in our business before we even figure out what this is."

They laughed, the sound mingling in the quiet room. As their laughter faded, a comfortable silence settled between them.

Ryan found himself studying Nina's face, memorizing the curve of her cheek and the way her eyes sparkled even in the dim light.

"You know what, Ryan?" Nina said. "I think the biggest pro is that we're here, having this conversation. We're both scared, but we're not running away."

Ryan nodded, feeling something warm unfurl in his chest. "You're right. And maybe that's enough for now. We don't have to have it all figured out."

CHAPTER 13

LATER THAT DAY, Ryan shifted in the living room lounge chair, where he'd parked after breakfast with Nina.

He'd convinced her to go tend the bakery, but she vowed to return soon. It bothered him that he was costing her business.

His knee throbbed, telling him it was time for another pain pill. The ice pack had long since melted, leaving a damp spot on his jeans. He glanced at the Christmas party to-do list on the side table, half of the items still unchecked.

Five days. He had five days until the event, and he could barely hobble to the bathroom without sweating. The barn remained undecorated, a cavernous space that needed filling.

"I can't do this." He rubbed his temples.

He reached for the budget spreadsheet, wincing as he leaned forward. Numbers swam before his eyes—deposits paid, balances due. Each figure represented a promise—to vendors, to the townsfolk, to the memory of his parents who'd started this whole tradition. Promises he couldn't keep.

The clock chimed, and Ryan's stomach clenched. Another hour gone. Another hour closer to what was shaping up to be a monumental disaster.

"I can't pull this off," he muttered.

Just then, the front door opened and Nina swept in. She'd changed clothes and now wore black leggings with a cute plaid skirt that showed off her shapely legs.

"I didn't knock," she explained as she walked down the hall. "Because I didn't want to make you get up—whoa!" She stopped short in the living room and stared at him. "What's wrong?"

Ryan pressed a palm to his nape. "I've got to cancel the party."

"What? Why?"

He waved a hand at his leg. "I can't even walk without crutches. The barn's empty. And

I've got five days to pull off a miracle. It's not happening."

"That's what you've got me for, silly." She set down the Ellis Early Eats bag she carried on the coffee table and came closer. The aroma of yeast bread scented the air.

"I can't ask you to shoulder that burden. It's not fair. We're not even..." He trailed off as his eyes met hers.

"Dating?" She arched an eyebrow.

"Well, yeah."

"Not yet," she said, "but we will be once the Christmas push is over."

But would they? Both of them worked sixty hours a week or more. When would they have time for each other? Ryan winced.

"We're not canceling the party," she said, her tone brooking no argument.

We. As if they were in this together.

His spirits lifted.

"Is this pain talking?" she asked. "When was the last time you took a pain pill?"

He shrugged. "Not since before you left."

She clicked her tongue, efficient, take charge. "First, let's take care of that."

Nina disappeared into the kitchen, taking the

bakery bag with her, and returned a few minutes later with his pill bottle and a glass of water. Like a diligent nurse, she waited for him to swallow the pill.

"Now," she said, sinking her hands onto her hips. "You listen to me, Ryan Danvers. This party isn't just about you. It's about the whole town. It's tradition. It's... it's Kringle! So no more self-pity. Got it?"

He loved the way her eyes sparkled when she was irritated with him. "I can't let—"

"No." She shook her head. "I won't hear 'can't.'"

"But—"

"No buts. You're not in this alone, you know. We can rally the troops. Get the whole town involved."

The idea of asking for help made Ryan's skin crawl. He'd always handled things on his own, especially after his parents died. The thought of admitting he couldn't do it all... "I can't ask people to do that. Everyone's busy with their own holiday stuff."

Nina snorted. "This *is* part of their holiday stuff, silly goose."

Ryan stared at her, a tiny spark of hope flickering to life in his chest. "You really think people would want to help?"

"Are you kidding? This party is the highlight of the year for half the town. They'd be thrilled to be part of making it happen." Nina grinned, nudging his shoulder. "Face it, Danvers. You're stuck with us."

"I don't know how to do this," he admitted, his voice low. "I've always... it's always been just me, well, except for Jenny and Scott, but this year, they can't help because of the baby."

Nina's expression softened. She reached out and touched his hand. "That's the point, Ryan. It doesn't have to be just you anymore. Let me help. Let me get the community involved. People love you. They loved your parents, and they've watched you struggle. They want to see you happy. They want to feel like they have a part in your healing."

"You think so?"

"I *know* so."

Ryan felt something shift inside him like a weight he'd been carrying for years rolled away. He took a deep breath, then nodded. "Where do we start?"

Nina's face lit up with a grin. "First things first.

We've got some calls to make. Operation Save Christmas is officially a go."

Pulling out her phone, Nina called Mrs. Claiborne first.

Ryan leaned back in his chair. For the first time in days, he felt a glimmer of real hope. Maybe this party could still happen. Not because of his stubborn determination to do it all alone but because of the very thing his parents had always cherished about Kringle—its sense of community, of family extending far beyond blood ties.

Nina hung up. "Mrs. Claiborne's on board. She's firing up the grapevine, and we'll have a crew here tomorrow. See how easy that was?"

"Hey," Ryan said. "Thank you. For not letting me give up."

Nina smiled, soft and warm. "That's what friends are for, right?"

Friends. Right.

Except Ryan was hoping for a whole lot more than that.

Four days had passed since Nina had reassured

Ryan about not canceling the Christmas party, and Kringle had turned into a Christmas wonderland.

Ryan's barn had become the heart of the community effort. This morning, when she left, twinkle lights hung from the rafters, fresh pine wreaths decorated the doors, and garlands draped along the walls. It felt magical, the kind of magic that only a small town at Christmas could create.

The townsfolk rallied together in a way that lifted Ryan's spirits. Upon his return, Scott took charge of organizing the volunteers. When she wasn't at the bakery, Nina spent hours working alongside the others at the ranch.

And then there was Ryan. His knee was healing faster than expected, and just yesterday, Nina drove him to the doctor for a checkup. The doctor had been pleased with his progress, and he was able to ditch the crutches, although Ryan still needed to wear the knee brace.

Today, on Christmas Eve eve, the bakery kitchen bustled too with party food prep. Gee and Jean Deerling worked together, making pies.

Their heads were close together, their hands moving in sync as they rolled out dough and cut perfect rounds to fit the pie tins. Jean's fingers expertly crimped the edges, creating neat, decorative crusts. Gee, for his part, was carefully slicing apples, piling the thin slices into the waiting shells.

Nina smiled. But as much as the sight of her grandfather falling in love lifted her spirits, there was a bittersweet edge to it. Watching them reminded her of the contrasts in her own world. Their relationship seemed so effortless, while her life felt tangled in complications—Ryan, the bakery, the looming decision. Part of her longed for that kind of clarity and peace, but it felt far away, hidden beneath the weight of everything she had to figure out.

But the weight of Katherine Brothers' offer gnawed at her. She hadn't told Ryan about the offer yet. Part of her didn't see the need—after all, they weren't officially together, and this was her decision to make. And he had enough on his mind with healing and putting on the party. Why complicate things right now?

Every time she thought about selling the bakery, her stomach twisted. Letting go of something her grandmother had built with her own hands felt wrong, like she was turning her back on a legacy. And yet the idea of stepping back, of having less responsibility and fewer sleepless nights was tempting.

Plus, there was Ryan. He was what she'd dreamed of for Christmas, and now, a relationship with him was completely within her reach.

A knock sounded at the back door.

Nina looked up. Who could that be this late in the evening? She wasn't expecting any deliveries.

Gee met her gaze, and they exchanged a glance. Nina wiped her hands on her apron and crossed the kitchen.

She peeked through the curtains.

Katherine Brothers stood on the threshold, her polished exterior as composed as ever. What did the woman want? Shouldn't she be home getting ready for her own celebration?

Nina opened the door. "Hello."

"Good evening, Nina. May I come in?"

She hesitated and then stepped aside. "All right."

"I hope I'm not interrupting." Katherine eyeballed Gee and Jean. "Nice to see you again, Mr. Ellis."

Gee raised a hand.

"We're baking for a Christmas party tomorrow, so we're short on time," Nina said. "What can we do for you? I'm guessing this visit isn't about pastries."

"It looks like you've got everything well in hand." Katherine offered a polite smile.

Nina gave the woman a pointed look.

"Yes, well, let me get to the point." Katherine cleared her throat. "If you want to sell the bakery, I need to know as soon as possible, or the offer goes away."

"I see."

"I know this isn't an easy decision for you, but you've had some time to think it over, and I've tried to be patient."

Nina's knee jerk reaction was to say no. She didn't like the woman's pressuring, but Katherine seemed sincere.

"When do you need an answer?"

"Tomorrow night."

Nina's gut twisted. Tomorrow night— Christmas Eve. The same night as the party. She pressed her lips together, glancing toward Gee and Jean, still working with quiet focus on their pies.

She knew what saying yes would mean. It wasn't just about stepping away from the bakery —it was about everything that came with that freedom. Freedom to live, to love, and to spend her days with Ryan without feeling torn between her responsibilities. Could it really be that simple? Just one decision and everything could change.

"I have been thinking about it," Nina said. "But it's not an easy decision."

Katherine's eyes softened. "I understand. Just remember, the offer expires after tomorrow night. If I don't hear from you, I'll assume your answer is no."

CHAPTER 14

THE BARN PULSED WITH LIFE, transformed from its usual rustic state into a festive wonderland. Garlands of fresh pine and holly adorned the weathered beams, their scent mingling with the aroma of cinnamon and spiced cider. Twinkling lights cascaded from the rafters, illuminating the gathered crowd.

His parents would have loved this!

Pride stoked his already happy mood. His knee, stabilized in a brace, was healing, and he'd traded in the crutches for a cane. He hadn't required a pain pill all day. He was running on adrenaline and excitement.

Ryan greeted guests as they arrived, shaking hands, accepting hugs, and fielding compliments about the festivities. He pointed people to the coat check and open bar. On the makeshift stage Scott had erected at the back of the barn, a local band was setting up.

Between the arriving invitees, he searched for Nina and found her arranging a tower of cupcakes at the dessert table. She wore a jade-green sweater that complemented her dark, glossy hair, which fell in soft waves around her shoulders.

She glanced up, met his gaze, and gave a soft smile.

For a second, it was just the two of them, and no one else in the barn existed. Nina wriggled her fingers, and his heart jumped.

He started toward her, compelled to be near Nina, but a group of new arrivals commanded his attention. When he looked up again, she was gone.

The band tuned up. Grown-ups chattered. Children darted between the adults, giggling as they played an impromptu game of tag.

In one corner, Garrett Ellis sat with Jean Deerling and a group of elders, sharing stories of Christmases past. Near the punch bowl, a cluster of teens giggled and shot shy glances at each other.

Mistletoe hung above the doorframes and dangled from the ceiling fans. Poinsettias brought a bright flourish of red to the proceedings, tugging at Ryan's memories. His mother had loved the Christmas flowers.

He ambled to the refreshment table where a couple of his high school buddies and their wives filled their plates. He talked with them for a few minutes, playing the dutiful host as his eyes scanned the room for Nina.

She'd been so busy they'd barely spoken over the last few days. He wanted to find her and tell her just how much he appreciated her. He poured himself a cup of hot apple cider and surveyed the crowd, his gaze landing on familiar faces—friends, neighbors, people who had known him his entire life.

This is how he remembered Christmas. Even the way his parents created and curated it over the years, bringing the community together to share in the joy of the season. It meant so much—not only to the townsfolk but to him as well.

Ryan was so glad Nina hadn't let him cancel. She was the real inspiration for this year's event. Because of her, it had happened.

"Quite a turnout, huh?" Scott's voice came from behind him.

Ryan turned to see his grinning brother-in-law. "Hey, man, thanks for your help."

"Always." Scott clamped him on the shoulder. "I was just FaceTiming with Jenny, showing off the party. She hates that she couldn't be here, but she's thrilled you're keeping up the tradition. It means a lot to her."

"How's she doing?"

"Going stir-crazy on bed rest. Jenny's already knitted three baby blankets. We're gonna have the warmest kid in town." Scott raised a hand in greeting to someone across the barn. "There's a customer I need to speak with. Talk to you later."

"Thanks again."

Ryan caught another glimpse of Nina. She was talking to a cluster of local women, her head thrown back, laughing at something one of them had said. His heart gave a tug. She'd come to mean so much to him in such a short amount of time, and he was so looking forward to taking their relationship deeper once the hustle and bustle of the holidays passed.

"Ryan! There you are!" Mrs. Claiborne's voice pulled him from his thoughts.

"Evening, Mrs. Claiborne. Thank you for

coming. The party's turning out pretty well, huh?" He smiled at her.

"Oh, it's simply wonderful! Everyone's having such a grand time. You've really outdone yourself this year," she said.

He gestured toward his bum knee. "I couldn't have pulled this off without Nina and help from the town."

"That Nina is a peach, isn't she?" Mrs. Claiborne's smile faded. "It'll be a lot quieter around here without her."

"Wait. What?" Ryan shook his head. Had he misheard? Highly possible since the band was playing "Jingle Bells" just a wee bit too loud.

Mrs. Claiborne leaned in closer and lowered her voice. "You haven't heard?"

"Heard what?" A surge of panic went through him. Was Nina okay?

Mrs. Claiborne gave him a sympathetic look. "Oh dear, I didn't mean to blindside you. I just assumed you knew since you and Nina are so close these days."

"Know what?" Suddenly, all the fantasies he'd been having of building a future with Nina vanished.

Mrs. Claiborne raised a hand. "I'm speaking

out of turn. Freddie says I never know when to keep my mouth shut, and he's right. Never mind me. I'm sure Nina will tell you about it after this hubbub dies down."

"Tell me about what?"

The older woman looked distressed. "Please don't say anything to Nina. I don't want her to be cross with me."

"Please, Mrs. Claiborne, you're scaring me. What's wrong?"

The older woman looked downright miserable at having unintentionally caused him distress. "Jean Deerling and I are good friends, and she was at the bakery last night helping Nina and Garrett get ready for the party when this city woman showed up and told Nina that she has one day to make up her mind about selling the bakery or her once-in-a-lifetime offer was going away."

Nina was considering selling the bakery and she hadn't said a word to him? The ground seemed to shift beneath him. Sell the bakery? The idea felt so foreign, so impossible. How had she not mentioned this to him? It wasn't just a business—Ellis Early Eats was her grandmother's legacy. The bakery was everything to her, just like the ranch was everything to him.

"She's considering selling?" he asked, hoping Mrs. Claiborne would correct herself.

"Well, it's a lot of money, Ryan," Mrs. Claiborne said. "Nina's a smart girl. I'm sure she'll make the right choice, whatever that may be, but she's always dreamed of traveling and seeing the world. I suppose an offer like that would give her the freedom to finally do it."

Travel. He remembered their conversation the night she slept in his bed—the night when he broke down about his parents' death—but he hadn't thought she was serious.

"I see." He paused. "Thanks for telling me, Mrs. Claiborne."

"Please don't tell Nina I spilled the beans. I'd hate for her to be cross with me."

"I won't say I heard it from you."

"Thank you. Now, I'm just going in for a kolach." She pressed past him to the buffet table. "It is a wonderful party, Ryan. Your parents would be so proud of you."

He wasn't listening to Mrs. Claiborne anymore. His gaze tracked across the barn until they found Nina again, still talking to the same group of women. She laughed at something one of them said, her smile as radiant as ever.

As if nothing had changed.

But everything had changed.

She didn't tell him. She'd been thinking about leaving, and she hadn't said a word. The weight of that realization pressed down on him, making the room feel smaller, the air suddenly thinner. Around him, the party continued—the chatter, the laughter, the music—but it all felt muffled, distant, as though he were standing on the outside looking in.

He watched as a child darted past, squealing in delight, nearly knocking over a tray of cookies. The band struck up another holiday tune, the lively notes filling the space, but none of it reached him. His world had narrowed to the ache in his chest and the question that wouldn't stop circling his mind. If she sold the bakery, was she leaving Kringle for good?

His knee throbbed, a dull pulse echoing the storm brewing inside him. People passed by. Some of them clapped him on the shoulder or offered a smile, but Ryan barely registered their faces. All the plans he'd started to make, the quiet hopes he'd dared to nurture, suddenly felt fragile—like ornaments on the edge of shattering.

Nina's laughter cut through the din, but

instead of drawing him in, it seemed to push him further away. The sight of her, standing there so effortlessly, made him feel... untethered. Like she was already slipping away, one foot already out the door.

A cold draft swept in through the barn doors, brushing past him, and Ryan shivered, though he wasn't sure if it was from the chill or the realization sinking into his bones. If this was what she wanted... if leaving was what would make her happy... He swallowed hard. He couldn't be the one to hold her back.

The party swirled around him, the barn alive with warmth and joy, but Ryan felt none of it. The music, the laughter, the twinkling lights—all of it seemed to blur at the edges like he was watching it through a fog.

And in that moment, surrounded by the people who had known him his whole life, Ryan had never felt more alone.

━━━

Holiday cheer filled the barn, but Nina's mind was elsewhere. By midnight, Katherine Brothers' offer would expire, and Nina had a serious choice to make. One that would alter the trajectory of her entire life.

That morning, a courier had arrived at Nina's door with a proposal package from Katherine—a detailed plan for the bakery that changed everything. The compendium wasn't just about the financial agreement for selling the bakery, but it was also a heartfelt tribute to Nina's grandmother, Ellie.

In Katherine's itemized strategy, the bakery would be renamed Ellie's, and new signage featured a vintage photo of Ellie in the kitchen. The logo took Nina's breath away. It was how she remembered her grandmother—smiling and holding a tray of cookies, resplendent in her element. The parcel included efforts for preserving Ellie's traditional recipes and restoration plans in keeping with the town's aesthetics, returning the bakery to its glory days.

It was sweet, it was sentimental, and it captured everything Kringle loved about the establishment.

And it moved Nina to tears.

Katherine understood what the bakery meant to the Ellis family, and that understanding made all the difference.

Before making a final decision, Nina had called her parents that morning, hoping for reassurance. She expected her father to feel conflicted, given that he had grown up in the bakery, but instead, his response was what she needed to hear.

"Nina," her father said, "your grandmother would be so proud of what you've done, but you don't have to keep holding on to the bakery just because it's been in the family for so long. You've already honored her legacy. This decision is yours, and whatever you choose, your mother and I are behind you."

Her parents' support eased some of the weight on her shoulders. She adored the bakery, and it held many fond memories, but the financial burden that came with it overwhelmed her. She worked seventy or eighty hours a week to keep Ellis Early Eats afloat.

Katherine's generous offer gave her a way to stay connected to her family's legacy without being swamped by the pressures of ownership. Nina would stay on to manage the bakery, but she would no longer be solely responsible for the business side. She would hire help to come in at three in the morning while she achieved a more balanced life.

There was just one more person she needed to speak to—Gee.

She spotted her grandfather sitting with Jean, smiling and chatting with their friends from the senior citizen center.

Gee caught her eye and gave her a wink.

Nina went over. "Enjoying the party?"

Gee's arm was around Jean's shoulder, and it lightened Nina's heart to see him so happy. It had been years since he'd smiled this much.

"Could I talk to you a sec?" she asked.

"Sure, sure." He stood up and dropped a kiss on Jean's upturned cheek. "Be back in a flash." Then he turned to Nina.

"Let's step outside," she said. "So we don't have to shout over the music."

They stepped outside, the December air nipping at their cheeks. Above them, stars lit up the calm night sky. Nina wrapped her arms around herself, feeling the weight of her decision lift.

"I wanted to let you know I've decided to sell the bakery. I'm going to call Katherine in a few minutes and let her know." Quickly, Nina told him about the new proposal Ms. Brothers had sent to her house.

"That sounds so wonderful," Gee said, his eyes

misting with tears. "The bakery will still honor your grandmother, but you'll be free of the heavy burdens of running a business."

"I talked to Dad and Mom earlier. Dad said he knows firsthand how hard it is to keep a small business going, and they support it. They'll be here for New Year's Eve as planned, and we can all say goodbye to the bakery as a family."

Gee looked sad, but he nodded. "It's time to let go of the past and embrace the future."

Nina swallowed hard, feeling shaky with so much emotion.

"No regrets, kiddo," Gee said and hugged her. "You've done more than anyone could have asked, Nina. You've honored your grandmother's legacy in every way, but love doesn't mean you have to hold on to something that's hurting you. Your grandmother would want you to be happy."

Tears pricked Nina's eyes as she wiped at them. "I just didn't want to feel like I was letting her down. Or you. Or Dad."

Gee hugged her again. "You're not letting anyone down. You've made us all proud. You're passing the bakery on to someone who will carry it forward, and that's a beautiful way to honor Ellie.

You're doing what's right for you, and that's what matters most."

For the first time in years, a sense of peace settled over Nina. Selling the bakery wasn't abandoning her family's legacy—it was ensuring that Ellie's spirit would live on while giving herself the freedom she needed. Katherine's plan would keep the heart of the bakery alive, and Nina would be there to see it without the constant weight of financial responsibility.

Now, there was only one more person to tell.

CHAPTER 15

BACK INSIDE, Nina escorted Gee to his table and then searched the crowded barn for one dear face among the sea of partygoers. The Christmas party was in full swing, laughter and chatter filling the air, but Nina couldn't shake the knot of anxiety in her stomach.

Where was Ryan?

He'd been right here, playing the host, but now he'd vanished.

She weaved through people, smiling politely at greetings but not stopping to chat. Her gaze darted from face to face, looking for Ryan's tall frame and warm brown eyes, but he was nowhere to be seen.

"Nina!" Scott's voice called out over the din. He approached, a glass of punch in hand. "Great party. Thank you so much for all you did helping Ryan this year."

"It was my pleasure," she said. "I couldn't have done it without the town pitching in. Have you seen Ryan, by the way?"

Scott pursed his lips. "Hmm, not for a while, but if I see him, I'll let him know you're looking for him."

She checked the refreshment tables and then the dance floor and finally poked her head into the old tack room converted into a coat check.

No Ryan.

Nina passed by a group of older women from her church and overheard a snippet of conversation.

"...selling the bakery," one of them whispered. "Can you believe it? After all these years..."

"I heard she's leaving town," another added. "Such a shame. That bakery's been a fixture in Kringle for generations."

Good grief. The grapevine had gone into hyperdrive. How had they found out so quickly? But if they knew, had Ryan also heard the rumor?

Where had he gotten off to?

Nina pushed open the barn doors and stepped out again. Strings of lights illuminated the guests huddled around the fire pit or heading to their cars. Was Ryan here bidding people good night?

She walked around the fire pit, anxious to see him, excited to tell him her big news, but didn't see him.

Had he gone to the house for something?

Turning, she was about to head for the farmhouse when she spied him leaning against the old oak tree next to the barn. His back was to her, shoulders tense under his jacket. Was his knee hurting him? Was that why he'd taken a break?

"Ryan," she called.

His shoulders stiffened, and he didn't turn around.

Alarm fled through her. "Ryan, you okay?"

Slowly, he rotated his body toward her, but his face stayed hidden in the shadows. "I'm fine."

"I've been looking for you."

Ryan stuffed his hands in his jacket pockets. "Yeah, it's been a busy night. Lots to do."

Nina frowned and walked closer. His tone was polite but distant. "Are you sure everything is okay? You seem..."

He shrugged, his gaze drifting past her to the people around the firepit. "Everything's fine. Just tired, I guess."

Nina searched his face. "No, it's more than that. What's going on?"

"It's nothing, Nina. Don't worry about it."

"It's not nothing. Talk to me, Ryan. Please."

He was silent for a long moment, his jaw clenching and unclenching. Finally, he met her gaze. "I heard about you selling the bakery, and I'm happy for you."

Nina's heart sank. What must he be thinking? "Oh, Ryan..."

"It's okay. I get it. This is your chance to see the world. Travel. Do the things you never got to do because you took over the family obligation. I just... I thought we had something going, but I understand. We've only been hanging out for two weeks, and I don't really figure into your plans."

"Leave Kringle?" Nina blinked, stunned. "Ryan, no. That's not—"

He held up a palm. "You don't have to explain. You've dreamed of traveling, of seeing the world. I don't want to hold you back. It's best to step away from our relationship now before..."

"Before what?" Nina asked, her heart racing.

Ryan's eyes met hers. "Before I fall any deeper."

Nina's breath caught in her throat. She

reached out, taking his hand in hers. "Oh, Ryan. You've got it all wrong."

He looked down at their joined hands and then back up at her. "What do you mean?"

"I'm not selling the bakery to leave," she explained, her voice trembling slightly. "I'm selling it so I can have time for *us*."

Ryan's eyes widened. "What?"

Nina took a deep breath and squeezed his hand. "The bakery has been my life. Every minute, every decision has revolved around it. And I love it, I do. But..." She paused, searching for the right words. "There's been no room for anything else. No room for me. No room for more."

A smile crept across his face. "So you're not leaving?"

Nina shook her head, a small smile tugging at her lips. "No, I'm staying. I'll still work at the bakery as the manager, but without the financial burden hanging over me. I'll still be part of it. I'm just making space for the things that matter."

"And what matters?" he asked.

Nina pressed a palm to his chest and felt the rapid beat of his heart that matched her own. "You. Us. The life we could build together, if... if that's what you want too."

For a moment, Ryan just stared at her, his eyes searching her face. Then he tugged her into his arms and held her close.

Nina melted into his embrace and buried her face against his chest.

"Really?" He exhaled.

"Really."

"I thought I was losing you," Ryan murmured against her hair. "I've been so afraid of that; I didn't even let myself hope..."

Nina pulled back to look up at him. "You're not losing me, Ryan. Not at all."

Ryan cupped her cheek and brushed his thumb across her skin. "I've wanted to get to know you better for years, but I was just in such a bad place after my parents died. I wasn't ready to move on. But now, this year, I've felt ready to live again, and when you invited me to dance that day in the bakery, I thought, well, maybe you wanted to get to know me better, too."

"It is what I want," Nina said, reaching up to trace her fingers over his beard stubble. "I want this. I want you. I want *us*."

They stood there for a moment, wrapped in each other's arms, the night air forgotten. The sounds of the party faded into the background, leaving just the two of them in their own little world.

Finally, Ryan pulled back slightly, a mischievous glint in his eye.

"Dance with me?" he asked softly.

Nina blinked, surprised. "Here? Now?"

Ryan nodded, already pulling her closer. He cocked his head toward the barn where the sounds of "Christmas Cookies" seeped through doors. "They're playing our song."

"But your knee—"

"Never mind that. Please, right here, under the stars. Just you and me."

She smiled up at him. "I'd love to."

They began to sway gently, barely moving. It wasn't a graceful dance—Ryan's knee made sure of that—but it was perfect in its own way. Overhead, the bright moon shone down on them. Nina rested her head on Ryan's chest and listened to the steady beat of his heart.

"Tell me something," Ryan said.

Nina lifted her head to look at him. "What?"

"Tell me about your dreams. The ones that don't involve the bakery."

She thought for a moment. "I've always wanted to learn how to paint. To capture the sunrise over the fields or the way the light hits the town square in the evening."

Ryan's smile deepened. "Really? That sounds amazing. I bet you'd be great at it."

Nina ducked her head, suddenly shy. "Maybe. What about you? What are your dreams?"

Ryan was quiet for a moment, his fingers tracing small circles on her back. "I've been thinking about doing more with the ranch. Maybe adding some educational programs, teaching kids about sustainable farming practices."

"That's a wonderful idea. The schools would love it, I bet."

"Yeah, but it's a big undertaking. I wasn't sure I could manage it all on my own, even with the help of my ranch hands. Scott and Jenny will be too busy raising their little one to pitch in much."

"You're not on your own anymore, Ryan," she said. "Whatever you need—whether it's help with the programs or just someone to bounce ideas off of —I'm here, and I can say that because I'll have time for the people I care about."

"I like the sound of that," he said. "And I'm here for you as well."

They fell silent again, continuing their slow swaying dance under the stars. Ahead of her lay a future she'd never dared to imagine before, but now it felt tantalizingly within reach.

"Oh!" Ryan said. "I almost forgot. I have something for you." He reached into his pocket, pulling out a small wrapped package.

Nina blinked in surprise. "Ryan, you didn't have to get me—"

"I wanted to. Open it."

Nina unwrapped the gift. Inside was a delicate silver charm in the shape of a whisk. She looked up at Ryan and laughed. "It's perfect."

"I bought it before I knew you were selling the bakery," he explained, "but I wanted you to have something to remember where you came from. The bakery might not be yours anymore, but the talent, the passion—that's all you, Nina."

Her eyes misted, and she clutched the charm to her chest, overwhelmed by his thoughtfulness. "I love it," she whispered. "Thank you."

"Merry Christmas, Nina," he murmured.

As they resumed their dance, a sense of peace settled over her. The anxiety and uncertainty that had plagued her melted away, replaced by hope and happiness.

She thought about the long road that had led her to this moment. The years of early mornings and late nights at the bakery, the weight of family legacy on her shoulders. She thought about the first time she'd really noticed Ryan—not just the handsome rancher, but as someone who saw her in a way no one else did.

And now, here they were, on the cusp of something new and wonderful.

"What are you thinking?" Ryan asked.

Nina smiled, tightening her arms around his neck. "Just... how lucky I am. How excited I am for the future."

Ryan's eyes crinkled at the corners as he smiled back. "Me too," he said. "I can't wait."

"Should we head back inside?" Nina asked, though she made no move to let go of Ryan. "Be sociable?"

He shook his head. "Not yet. Let's stay here a little longer. Just us."

Nina looked at Ryan. His eyes met hers, dark with desire. Without a word, he pulled her close, one hand on her waist, the other intertwining with her fingers.

They moved, not to the faint music from the barn, but to a rhythm all their own. Ryan dipped his head, and when his lips met hers in a searing kiss, she melted into him.

Ryan's arms tightened around her, and she slid her free hand up to tangle in his hair. They swayed together, lost in the taste and feel of each other. The kiss deepened, hungry and passionate, full of beautiful nights to come.

When they finally parted, both were breathless. Ryan rested his forehead against hers, their bodies pressed together.

As snowflakes began to drift down around them, Nina knew she would remember this precious moment forever.

It was, without a doubt, a perfect Christmas dance.

EPILOGUE

The barn at the Double D ranch was alive with conversation and music. Tables lay spread with Christmas cookies, pies, canapés, and mugs of cider. The sounds of laughter, toasts, and clinking glasses resounded. Neighbors moved between groups, exchanging holiday greetings, while the band played "All I Want for Christmas Is You."

Nina stood near the entrance, taking in the scene. This year's Christmas Eve party felt different, more connected. The entire town pitched in, helping to fund the event, lightening the load on Ryan and making the evening feel like a true community celebration.

She spotted her parents seated with Gee and Jean who'd married two months ago. Her father was in full storytelling mode, his hands moving with every word, while her mother sat back, smiling quietly, enjoying the show. Gee laughed, leaning into Jean, more relaxed than Nina had seen him in years. She was so happy he'd found love again.

Seeing them together, Nina felt a deep peace. It had been a whirlwind year full of changes, but here they all were, celebrating together. Gee and her parents had been there for her through every transition, from selling the bakery to embracing her new role as manager, and now, they were here to celebrate.

Not far off, Jenny chased after her son, Adam, who was on a determined mission to grab another Christmas ornament off the tall Scotch pine. Scott followed, laughing as Jenny scooped Adam up just before he could get into trouble.

Nearby, Mrs. Claiborne, wrapped in her festive red shawl, was in conversation with a group of neighbors. She had always been a constant in Kringle, offering advice whether asked for or not, and today, her approval seemed evident in the brief nod she gave Nina from across the room.

Ryan appeared at Nina's side, slipping his hand into hers.

"Ready for a dance?" he asked, his tone easy, although there was a hint of something more in his eyes. "I asked the band to play "Christmas Cookies."

Nina smiled. "I'm always ready to dance with you."

The band shifted into George Strait's holiday ditty. Ryan led her to the center of the barn, guiding her smoothly across the floor. His knee had fully healed, and they often went dancing on Friday nights. His hand was steady at her back, and they danced as if they were made for each other, which, hey, they were.

When the song was over, the band stopped playing, and everyone left the dance floor. Nina started to head back to their table, but Ryan didn't let go of her hand and instead tugged her back toward him.

The look in his eyes sent her heart skipping. "What is it?"

"This," he said and lowered himself to one knee.

Nina put a palm to her mouth as the hand he held on to trembled.

The barn fell quiet.

From his pocket, Ryan pulled out and opened a small velvet box, his eyes never leaving hers.

"Nina," he said, his voice strong and sure, "you've been my partner through everything this past year. I couldn't imagine going through life without you. I want to spend every Christmas and every day with you for the rest of my life. Will you marry me?"

For a moment, the world around them faded and she nodded as happy tears filled her eyes. "Yes, Ryan. Of course, I'll marry you."

Applause broke out from the guests, along with cheers and catcalls. Ryan stood, sliding the ring onto her finger. "You've made me the happiest guy in the world!"

Nina glanced around the barn, catching sight of her parents. Her mother dabbed her eyes with a tissue while her father raised his glass in a small toast.

Jenn beamed at Nina and Ryan. Gee and Jean exchanged a look. Their hands were still clasped together, their own love story having unfolded this past year, too. And Mrs. Claiborne, standing off to the side, gave Nina a brief approving smile as if everything had fallen exactly into place.

And indeed, it had.

Dear Reader,

Thank you so much for reading *A Perfect Christmas Dance*. If you enjoyed Ryan and Nina's story, I would so appreciate a review. You have no idea how much it means to us! Readers rock!

If you'd like to keep up with my latest releases, you can sign up for my newsletter @ https://loriwilde.com/subscribe/ To check out other books, you can visit me on the web @ www.loriwilde.com.

To keep up with books that go on sale, follow me on Bookbub for free or .99 cent book deals. bookbub.com/profile/lori-wilde.

You can also join my reader group on Facebook @ https://www.facebook.com/groups/452076275271253 to enter for giveaways and book bargains.

Wishing you much love and light!
    —Lori

ABOUT THE AUTHOR

Lori Wilde is the *New York Times, USA Today,* and *Publishers' Weekly* bestselling author of 110 works of fiction. A three time Romance Writers of America RITA finalist, she has four times been nominated for Romantic Times Readers' Choice Award. She has also won numerous other awards, sold over ten million books worldwide, and inspired seven Hallmark movies, including, *A Kismet Christmas,* based on her breakout book. Lori loves helping writers achieve their publishing dreams.

ALSO BY LORI WILDE

KRINGLE, TEXAS

A Perfect Christmas Gift

A Perfect Christmas Wish

A Perfect Christmas Surprise

A Perfect Christmas Joy

A Perfect Christmas Reunion

A Perfect Christmas Kiss

A Perfect Christmas Dance

CHRISTMAS BEACH

Christmas Beach Wedding

Christmas Beach Proposal

Christmas Beach Reunion

TEXAS RASCALS SERIES

Keegan

Matt

Nick

Kurt

Tucker

Kael

Truman

Dan

Rex

Clay

Jonah

ROAD TRIP RENDEZVOUS SERIES

The Joan Wilder Effect

The Las Vegas Effect

The Thomas Crowne Effect

The Mummy Effect

COWBOY COUNTRY SERIES

Montana Blaze

Arizona Heat

Texas Sizzle

With Kristin Eckhardt

COWBOY CONFIDENTIAL

Cowboy Cop

Cowboy Protector

Cowboy Bounty Hunter

Cowboy Bodyguard

Cowboy Outlaw

THE COWBOYS OF CALAMITY, TEXAS

Noah

Ben

Will

With Pam Andrews Hanson

WRONG WAY WEDDING SERIES

The Groom Wager

The DIY Groom

The Stand-In Groom

The Royal Groom

The Makeshift Groom

Made in United States
Cleveland, OH
06 March 2026